WHITE HOUSE
CLUBHOUSE

WHITE HOUSE
CLUBHOUSE

SEAN O'BRIEN

Norton Young Readers
An Imprint of W. W. Norton & Company
Celebrating a Century of Independent Publishing

For Erin, Jay, and Clare

For information about permission to reproduce selections from this book, write to
Permissions, W. W. Norton & Company, Inc., 500 Fifth Avenue, New York, NY 10110

For information about special discounts for bulk purchases, please contact
W. W. Norton Special Sales at specialsales@wwnorton.com or 800-233-4830

Manufacturing by Lakeside Book Company
Book design by Hana Anouk Nakamura
Production manager: Delaney Adams

ISBN 978-1-324-05292-0

W. W. Norton & Company, Inc., 500 Fifth Avenue, New York, N.Y. 10110
www.wwnorton.com

W. W. Norton & Company Ltd., 15 Carlisle Street, London W1D 3BS

1 2 3 4 5 6 7 8 9 0

WHITE HOUSE
CLUBHOUSE

CHAPTER 1

THE TREE

MARISSA felt a tap on her elbow. She tried to ignore it.

The equations on the board made no sense. She felt so behind.

New math. New school. New city. New house.

And not just any house. The White House.

Washington, DC, was colder than California. Moving right after a blizzard didn't help. They had to bring in bulldozers to move the snow for Mom's inaugural parade. That was January. Now it was March. The cherry blossoms were still frozen.

Another tap. Liza was trying to pass a note.

Liza was OK, Marissa guessed. She didn't act weird around Marissa like the other fifth graders. She didn't care that Marissa's mom was the president. She never giggled and pointed when Big Dan peeked in the window of the class door to make sure Marissa was still breathing. She didn't ask why Marissa wasn't allowed to eat school lunch or trade food or treats.

Marissa nervously tugged at the red-and-black friendship bracelet on her wrist. The one Emily gave her back in Sacramento, before the big move. Emily had a bracelet just like it. But she wasn't wearing it in her latest posts.

Liza tapped one more time. When Mr. Shapiro faced the board to write something else, Marissa turned and took the note from Liza.

It said: *Pick a color—purple, blue, red, or orange.*

Marissa circled red with her pencil and crumpled the note in her hand, then she pretended to scratch the back of her neck as she dropped the note onto Liza's desk behind her.

She could hear Liza whispering "R-E-D" as she moved her fingers back and forth in the paper fortune-teller she had made.

Another note: *Pick a number—1, 3, 5, or 7.*

Marissa circled 7 and dropped it back. She heard the four points of Liza's fortune-teller rustle back and forth seven times.

2, 4, 6, or 8? read another note.

8, Marissa wrote back.

She heard Liza opening one of the corners and smoothing out the paper.

Liza leaned forward and slid the open fortune-teller under Marissa's arm onto her notebook. Marissa looked down and read her fortune: *You will go on a crazy cool adventure!*

Marissa rolled her eyes. Marissa was so tired of everyone saying things like that to Marissa and her younger sister, Clara. Living in the White House must be such an adventure!

More like permanent detention.

Every minute, of every day, Marissa was being watched.

Going to the mall—now *that* would be an adventure.

She hadn't done that since Christmas.

Walk down the street by herself? Not in over a year.

A moment later a piece of paper poked her elbow.

"Liza!" Mr. Shapiro barked from the front of the class. "How many times have I told you not to pass notes?"

"Uh . . ." stammered Liza.

"It was me," said Marissa. "I started it."

"Oh," said Mr. Shapiro, sounding surprised and flustered. "Well then, uh, please . . . don't."

The bell rang, and the class exploded into noise.

Marissa stayed in her seat as everyone else left.

On her way out the door, Liza looked at Marissa and mouthed "thank you."

When the classroom was empty, Big Dan stuck his clean-shaven head in the door and said, "Ma'am, are you ready?"

Ma'am. Who calls an eleven-year-old "ma'am"? Back in California they didn't even call Marissa's mother ma'am. Or Mrs. or Ms. or madam. Sometimes people called her "Governor Suarez." Sometimes they called Marissa's dad "Major Suarez." But most of the time it was just Julia and Ricardo. That's just how people were in California. They liked first names there. And they didn't like to wear ties or sit in offices. They got outside.

Marissa missed the family bike trips in the Sierras, where Mom grew up. On those long, misty rides, Marissa's sister Clara had to climb every rock and tree she could, but Marissa just wanted to explore. If she saw a path, she just had to follow it.

That's how she'd found the giant.

It was off the path, deep in the woods. Marissa saw an old, blackened chimney by a creek and wanted to explore. Just the ruins of an old cabin. But then she saw the tree. The biggest one she had ever seen. She ran up for a closer look and found herself in front of a wall of rippled bark so wide she couldn't take it all in, a tree so tall its branches seemed to brush against the clouds. At the top was a thick crown of green, so old it seemed to be whispering secrets from centuries back as the mountain wind passed through it.

Creaking, waving, whispering. There was a cave, right through the base of the tree. It was a narrow triangular passage, somehow carved out of the wood of the big tree. It was dark and overgrown, with daylight peeking through from the other side. Marissa crawled in, making her way to the middle of the tree where a wide-open space opened up, dark and sooty. She leaned against the moist wood and closed her eyes.

She was relaxed.

She was happy.

"Ma'am?" Big Dan said again.

She was late.

"The cars are all lined up," said Big Dan, "engines running."

"That's so bad for the environment," Marissa grumbled.

"That's why I said it, ma'am," Big Dan said with a little smile. "I knew it would get you moving."

Marissa gave him a look, picked up her bag, and followed him out of the classroom. They walked downstairs to Clara's third-grade classroom.

The door was open. The only student left was Clara.

And she was on the top shelf of the bookcase.

"Ma'am, you will give me a heart attack someday," said Big Dan.

"Come on down, Clara," said Marissa.

Clara scowled, then leapt from the top shelf onto the carpet below, landing in perfect form. She grabbed her book bag and skipped out of the classroom.

"Sierra and Sugar en route school bus," Big Dan whispered into his sleeve as they went down another flight of stairs and out the side entrance, where three large black SUVs were parked. The engines were running. Always ready to escape danger. Or something.

When the heavy doors clunked the girls safely into their car, Big Dan got into the front seat and picked up the radio.

"Shadow copy," he said. "School bus departing Textbook, status bravo."

The lead car pulled out in front of them, and the other pulled out behind. Marissa and Clara's car pulled in between them and the car parade began, speeding through the streets of Washington with three police motorcycles in front and another three behind. At one point the car parade zipped across the double yellow lines and sped down the wrong side of the street.

"Counterflow, baby!" Clara cried out enthusiastically.

She waved at the people staring from the sidewalk. Marissa sank lower in her seat.

"Shadow copy," Big Dan said into the radio as the car parade approached the White House. "School bus arriving Crown. Sierra and Sugar are green."

They made a sharp left turn off 17th Street and clattered over a set of metal plates by the guard shack on E Street. The motorcycles sped away, while the cars made another sharp left turn past the iron gates, and over more metal plates onto State Place.

The drive was lined with hundreds of different flags.

"What's that for?" asked Clara.

"Tonight's the state dinner, remember?" said Marissa.

The cars entered one more set of iron gates and slowly circled the drive around the South Lawn of the White House.

"Do we have to go?" asked Clara.

"Of course we have to go!" Marissa said as the cars pulled to a stop. "Don't you ever look at the calendar?"

Clara glared at her sister and tugged impatiently at the door handle.

"You have to wait for Dan," said Marissa.

"*I know,*" growled Clara.

As soon as Big Dan opened the door, Clara bolted across the South Lawn and started climbing an old oak tree.

Big Dan whispered into his sleeve, "Code yellow South Lawn." He started walking quickly but smoothly toward Clara's tree. "Sugar is yellow. Repeat, yellow."

Multiple uniformed officers in white shirts slid into position along the south fence and started gesturing for all the tourists to move back.

Marissa watched all of this happening through the tinted window of the SUV. She shook her head and took Clara's backpack as well as her own, then carried them into the West Wing.

She peeked into the Oval Office, but Mom wasn't there. Her voice was coming from behind a closed door leading to the small dining room. The one they called the Oval Office Dining Room. Because that's what it was. So original.

Marissa felt eyes watching her. She turned and saw the portrait of a frowning face with a red mustache and sharp eyes, glaring down from a frame just inside the Roosevelt Room. This place was like a haunted house, with all the creepy portraits. Marissa trudged past several other dead presidents on her way across the lobby and up the red carpet stairs to the family residence.

As she stepped into the upper hallway, she tripped on something round and crashed to the floor, sending both backpacks flying. She stood up and turned to see what she'd tripped on. Clara's red soccer ball, the one she'd gotten from the Women's World Cup team when they came to visit.

Marissa gave the ball a frustrated kick. It slammed into the top shelf of a bookcase, knocking an old blanket to the floor. The ball flew back at Marissa with surprising speed, bouncing down the stairs and across the marble floor of the lobby below. Marissa chased the ball into the State Dining Room, watching helplessly as it hurtled toward an old side table with wooden eagle legs, covered with fragile wineglasses. Marissa closed her eyes, waiting for the crash. Nothing happened. Marissa opened her eyes. The wineglasses were still there.

But the ball was gone.

Marissa searched. She looked under every table decorated with little flags, under every window, behind every curtain. She even looked in the fireplace under Abraham Lincoln's portrait. She couldn't find the ball.

Marissa went back to the wooden eagle table and crouched below it to see if it was hidden below. As she leaned in for a closer look, her shoulder bumped one of the wooden wings.

The wing snapped back like a switch, and a panel opened in the wall. Inside was a narrow tunnel, and there was the ball. Marissa reached for the ball but she couldn't quite get it. She crawled in a little farther, but when she touched the ball it rolled away into the darkness.

She tried to back her way out. But she was stuck.

CHAPTER 2

THE NEWSPAPER

OUT on the South Lawn, Clara climbed higher into her favorite tree as Big Dan watched from below. As she neared the top, Clara felt a shape carved into the trunk.

It felt like a letter *O*, overgrown and faded, carved a long time ago. Clara ran her hand over the bark next to the shape and found another one right next to it—the letter *R*. Next to the *R* was a *C*, and an *S*.

"ORCS," Clara said out loud, wondering what it meant. She looked down at all the Secret Service agents on the ground. None of them had ever climbed this tree. Nobody knew about ORCS. For once, a secret was hers. Maybe she'd tell Marissa.

Clara climbed down and ran into the White House. She smelled sugar cookies. She went into the State Dining Room in hopes of sneaking one before the big dinner.

"Help!"

Clara heard her sister, but she couldn't see her.

Then she spotted a pair of sneakers sticking out of the wall.

"You found a secret passage!" Clara cried in delight.

"Get me out of here," said Marissa. "I'm hanging over some kind of old slide."

"Cool!"

"Not cool. Who knows where this thing ends up."

Clara tried pulling Marissa's feet but she couldn't get her out. She tried pushing.

And Marissa shot forward into the darkness.

Clara peeked into the tunnel. "Oops," she said quietly.

"I'm OK," said Marissa's voice, from a long distance away. "There's a door down here."

"*Nice!*" exclaimed Clara. She jumped through the panel and flew down the slide, spiraling down into the darkness. She crashed into Marissa and rolled onto a stone floor.

In front of her was a door, with a faint light coming through the cobwebbed gap at the bottom. Clara found the iron doorknob and pushed the door open an inch. It creaked against rusty hinges. There was a clatter in the room beyond, followed by the sound of frantic footsteps.

"Hello?" Clara called. No response. "Anybody home?"

After listening for a while longer, Clara gave the door another push. The old door creaked the rest of the way open, revealing a large oval room filled with old furniture and toys.

Candles flickered along the rainbow-colored wall, giving the room a warm, inviting glow. The wall was lined with doors, most of them covered with dust and cobwebs as if they hadn't been opened in years.

But across the room was one door that was slightly open.

Near this door was a child-sized wooden chair, toppled over on its side. Next to the chair was a crisp white newspaper open to the comics page. Some of the pictures on the page had been colored in, and several crayons were scattered on the floor nearby.

"Look, it's a kids' room!" exclaimed Clara, sprinting into the room and jumping on one of the old couches.

There were little toy animals and wooden games all around the room. Tin soldiers stood at attention in front of an overstuffed couch. An artist's easel leaned against the wall, surrounded by a pile of paintbrushes.

While Clara bounced from couch to couch, Marissa headed for the bookcase, its shelves sagging with the weight of dozens of old books. *Treasure Island. Little Women. Gulliver's Travels*. Marissa ran her fingers along the faded leather spines, stopping at a tan book with a gold ink picture of an Egyptian sphinx with wings. *The Time Machine*, by H. G. Wells.

"Check out these clothes!" exclaimed Clara, flicking through old-fashioned dresses on a rack near the wall. "Come on, let's try them on!"

"Maybe we shouldn't," said Marissa, but Clara had already kicked off her sneakers and was changing into a maroon dress.

Marissa shook her head disapprovingly, then saw a dark green dress that looked just her size. She walked over and picked it up.

"Come on," said Clara, skipping around the room in her bare feet and her new old dress. "You know you want to."

Marissa looked again. It really was a pretty dress. Dusty, a little worn out, and complicated, with petticoats and everything.

"All right," said Marissa. "Maybe we can show up for the state dinner looking like we just robbed the Smithsonian."

"Yeah!" said Clara, doing a cartwheel.

As Marissa struggled into the strange old dress, Clara picked up the newspaper.

"These comics are weird," said Clara. "'Jubilant Jerry Opens a Matrimonial Bureau'?"

"Is that the *Post*?" asked Marissa.

"No, it's"—Clara turned to the front page and read—"the *San Francisco Call*."

"Let me see that," said Marissa, finally making it into the dress.

"All yours," said Clara, flinging the paper toward her sister, scattering its pages across the floor.

"Thanks," Marissa said sarcastically.

She walked over, her bare feet cold against the stone floor. As she picked up the comics, the opposite side of the page caught her eye. There was a black-and-white photograph of a tree stump, with little blurred shadows that looked like fairies dancing across the top of it in white dresses and black tuxedos.

As Marissa looked closer at the picture, she realized the little shadows weren't fairies at all—they were real people, dancing on a stump of such a massive scale it just made them look tiny.

The headline read: "Revel in the Woods: Wendell Corporation Hosts Society Ball on Future Dam Site."

Marissa held the paper up in the flickering candlelight and continued reading: "Top executives at the Wendell Corporation threw a grand affair for the cream of San Francisco society in the Sierra foothills to celebrate the start of construction on the Wendell Dam. When completed, this dam will flood the valley and provide San Francisco with sufficient electricity to make it a true city of the future."

Marissa's eyebrows furrowed. Did her mom know about this?

"The land," the article went on, "site of a giant sequoia forest, was cleared with much heroic effort by company founder Arnold Wendell. Several of the felled trees measured in excess of twenty feet in diameter and are estimated to have been over a thousand years old. One of the largest trees yielded a stump of sufficient size to be used as a dance floor."

"Marissa, check this out!" Clara called from across the room.

"Hang on," Marissa responded, getting angry at the blurry little people in the picture. There was another photograph farther down the page, taken at a distance. The stump the people danced on was surrounded by other stumps, some just as big. A whole forest of ancient big trees, wiped out.

Except for one.

Near the dance floor stood a tall, thick tree. At first Marissa thought it was the same tree she'd crawled into in California. But then she saw that its base was solid all the way around. There was no tunnel. And at the top, a narrow spire stuck up through the thick crown of branches, making it look like an upside-down ice cream cone.

"Revelers were also afforded the opportunity to say goodbye to a California landmark," the article continued. "The famed Steeple Giant sequoia, three hundred feet in height and two thousand years of age, will be the last to go when dam construction necessitates its harvesting."

Unlike the first picture, this one was in sharp focus, and clear contrast. She could almost hear the wind rustle through its high branches. Whispering. Creaking. Swaying.

"Hey!" yelled Clara. "I called you like a million times."

"Oh . . . sorry . . ." said Marissa absently. She didn't care what her sister had to show her. She only cared about that one tree, the last one standing. "I gotta go show this to Mom."

"Mom's busy," said Clara.

"I don't care." Marissa looked at the date on the front page of the paper. March 1. "This thing is already a few weeks old!"

Marissa's pulse quickened. Maybe they were already chopping the tree down.

"What thing?" Clara said, skipping over. She grabbed the paper from Marissa. Her eyebrows lifted and she carefully handed it back. "It's more than a few weeks old."

Marissa looked again at the date. March 1, 1903.

She looked again at the picture and saw the old-fashioned clothes on the tiny people. The paper looked new, but it must have been lying around in the room for over a century. The tree was surely gone by now.

"Forget that," said Clara. "I found something even cooler."

Marissa tucked the newspaper page into her pocket, then followed Clara to a wooden table against the wall. Between two candles on the table was a large piece of weathered parchment, covered in small handwriting, like the Declaration of Independence. There was an inkwell and a feather quill sitting next to it.

"'White House . . . Clubhouse,'" Clara read. "'To whom it may concern. If you are reading this, you are one of us. A White House kid.'"

The girls looked at each other.

Clara read the next paragraph. "'You belong here. White House kids are never alone. By signing below, we promise to help each other, because we're the only ones who understand what it's like to live here. We promise to help the president, because nobody's perfect (especially grown-ups). And we promise to make a difference, because we can. Will you accept the mission?'"

Below these words were dozens of signatures. Some were names she'd never heard of, but others had familiar last names. Tad Lincoln. Jesse Grant. Charlie Taft. In the corner near the bottom someone had written the word *Roosevelt* in elegant flowing letters, and six names surrounded it in different handwriting. *Alice. Ted. Kermit. Ethel. Archie.* And in a shaky childish scrawl, *Quentin.*

"I want to sign!" said Clara, grabbing the quill from the inkwell.

"Hold on," said Marissa. "This is really old, don't you think this belongs in a museum?"

"It belongs to us!" said Clara. "We're White House kids, right?"

She dipped the quill and wrote her name, leaving a trail of dripping ink. She handed the quill to Marissa, then skipped over to one of the couches and dove into a headstand on the cushions.

"Woo-hoo!" she said upside down. "Our very own clubhouse!"

Marissa looked at the quill in her hand. The feathers quivered as a light breeze passed through the room. What did all this mean?

You belong here, the document said.

Not really, thought Marissa. The whole thing felt like a lie. Just like that first day when she walked upstairs in the White House, two hours after her mother's inauguration, and saw all their family pictures already stuck to the wall, and all her stuff neatly unpacked in a narrow bedroom with its own fireplace.

Marissa saw the upside-down eyes of her sister, watching her expectantly. Marissa looked at the quill. She dipped it in the ink. She took a breath and wrote her name.

A sharp gust of wind swept across the room, scattering the newspaper and knocking over several tin soldiers. The candles went out. Everything went dark. A door slammed shut.

CHAPTER 3

THE PONY

MARISSA stared into the void, willing her eyes to adjust. The air was still. The dark was total.

"Marissa?" whispered Clara.

"Yeah."

"No one knows we're down here."

"I know," said Marissa. She stepped blindly to her left and bumped into the table.

"I mean, what if—"

"I know, Clara."

Marissa moved along the table's edge until she found the wall. She ran her fingers along the smooth plaster until it was interrupted by a door. She felt for the doorknob and tried to turn it. But it wouldn't budge.

"I want to go home," said Clara's voice from across the dark room.

Marissa blindly moved along to the next door, feeling the thick cobwebs and dust lining the wood. She tried this one as well, with no luck. She reminded herself that there were lots of doors lining the wall. Running her hand along the oval wall, she found the next door. And the one after that. And the one after that. None would open.

Her heart was racing now, her breathing shallow and tight. She bumped into the bookcase and heard several books fall to the floor. She tried three more doors, pulling and pushing harder and harder on every one. She smacked a door in frustration, producing a cloud of dust that triggered a coughing fit. Marissa sat on the floor and leaned against the wall.

A hand touched her shoulder.

"AAH!" said Marissa.

"It's just me!" whispered Clara.

Marissa exhaled. "Sorry."

She took Clara's hand. Together they worked their way to the next door. Marissa pushed against it. It held strong. So did the next one.

But the one after that was already slightly open.

Marissa gave Clara's hand a reassuring squeeze and went through the doorway.

"What about our clothes?" asked Clara. "And our shoes?"

"We can come back with a flashlight," whispered Marissa. "Let's just get out of here."

In the darkness she found the bottom of the slide. She managed to get up about five feet before her feet slipped out from under her and she slid back down, crashing into Clara.

Clara pushed past her and easily scampered up the slide.

"That's what happens when you spend all your playground time reading," she called down from the top of the slide.

"Shut up," said Marissa. "Can you get out?"

"Yeah, it's open," said Clara. Then she cried, "Moose!"

"What?" asked Marissa, huffing her way to the top. Marissa crawled out of the passage, careful not to bump the wooden eagle because she knew there were fragile wineglasses on top.

Except there weren't.

When Marissa stood up, she saw the table held only a silver tea set, with a bowl filled with sugar cubes. The other tables were gone. No fancy dishes. No little flags.

In fact, the whole room seemed different. There was green fabric all over the place. And where Abe Lincoln's portrait was supposed to be, there was a big tapestry of a forest.

"Moose!" Clara exclaimed again, standing in the middle of the room.

Marissa looked up. The head of a giant moose loomed over the fireplace. Its wide, flat antlers stretched out in both directions, and there were large black marbles where its eyes were supposed to be. On either side of the moose were the heads of bighorn sheep. More heads lined the ceiling: a deer with sharp antlers, a buffalo with empty eyes, a jaguar with glimmering teeth.

"What did they do to our house?" asked Clara in a shaky voice.

Marissa shook her head in shock. "Did Mom lose her mind while we were down there?"

"I don't like this place," said Clara, looking at a bearskin rug mounted on the wall with the head still on it. Its mouth hung open in a mute roar.

"They're stuffed," Marissa said.

"They're scary!" said Clara.

"Yeah, but..." Marissa looked around, trying to find something to calm her sister down.

"How about this little guy?" she said, leading Clara to a small furry creature on the mantel. "Don't you think he's cute?"

Clara looked at its beady little black eyes, its lifelike whiskers, its long, fluffy fur streaked with brown and black. Its front paws were raised together, like little hands forever suspended in silent prayer.

Then its head moved.

"GAH!" yelled Clara.

The animal skittered off the mantel. Clara ran the other way.

"Let's get out of here!" Clara shouted, running back to the wooden eagle table and accidentally knocking some sugar cubes onto the floor. She pounded on the wall under the table. "What happened to the door?"

Marissa didn't answer. She was staring at the doorway.

A boy, no more than eight years old, stared back.

Clumps of red hair stuck out from under his wool cap, and his white shirt, gray vest, and short, puffy pants were stained with grass and mud.

"Hello?" said Marissa cautiously.

The boy kept staring.

"Was that your . . . hamster?" asked Marissa.

"Guinea pig," the boy corrected her, his eyes darting back and forth between Marissa and Clara. "Admiral Dewey. We have lots of guinea pigs. Doctor Johnson. Bishop Doane. Father O'Grady. And Fighting Bob Evans," said the boy. "That's Father's favorite. He sits on Father's desk upstairs."

"Upstairs?" asked Marissa. She didn't know everyone working in the White House, but she was pretty sure she knew everyone with access to the family residence.

"Who is your father?" she asked suspiciously.

"Teddy!" said the boy.

A distant train whistle wailed beyond the open window. A horse neighed close by.

"Teddy who?" asked Marissa.

The boy gave her a funny smile, as if he thought she was crazy. "Everybody knows Teddy!"

"Well, I don't," answered Marissa.

"Teddy *Roosevelt*?" said the boy, rolling his eyes.

"What?" asked Clara from under the table.

Marissa cautiously took the newspaper page out of her pocket and unfolded it. March 1, 1903. The paper was crisp and new.

"That's mine!" the boy said. He ran over and pointed at the crayon marks on the newspaper. "I was coloring it in when . . ."

He looked at Marissa. His eyebrows shot up. "That was *you*!" He grinned, revealing two missing front teeth. "You came from the clubhouse!"

Clara emerged from under the table. "And *you* knocked over the chair and ran away!"

"I did! I did!" said the boy, looking at Clara and bouncing up and down in excitement. "I was by myself in the clubhouse, because my brother Archie is sick and he can't play, and my other brothers Kermit and Ted are at boring school—"

"Boring school?" asked Clara.

"Not boring school," the boy said impatiently, "*Bor*ing school!"

"Boarding school," said Marissa.

"Right!" the boy said, trying to enunciate against the gap in his teeth. "Boring school!"

"And my sister Ethel says I'm annoying," the boy continued, "and my other sister Alice is almost a grown-up because she had a different mother—"

"Quentin," said an elegant female voice, "is there any more of my personal business you'd like to spill to wandering strangers?"

A beautiful young woman walked through the lobby doorway. Her old-fashioned dress was light blue, with a high laced collar that went right up to her chin.

"Hullo, Alice!" Quentin said. He put one hand next to his mouth and loudly whispered, "They're from the clubhouse!"

Alice nodded thoughtfully. "Pleasure to make your acquaintance, ladies. I assume you know your way around already."

There was a thump. Alice cast a disapproving glance over to Quentin, then said, "Though I'd advise you to keep an eye out for animals running wild."

"They met Admiral Dewey already," said Quentin.

"I'm not talking about rodents, little brother," said Alice.

There was another neigh.

"I was just trying to cheer Archie up!" said Quentin.

"Quentin," said Alice disapprovingly, "what did Mother Edith say about taking our little pets into the house?"

"You do it all the time!" said Quentin, gesturing at Alice's purse.

"Emily Spinach is family," answered Alice, pulling a small green snake from inside her purse and cradling it in her hands. "And a snake is hardly the same as a pony."

"But Archie hasn't rode Algonquin since he got the measles, and I thought, but then I couldn't get him up the stairs, and . . ."

Quentin's voice trailed away. He turned and walked sadly toward the door leading to the Red Room.

"Okaaaay," he said as he disappeared through the doorway.

"There's really a horse in there?" asked Marissa.

"Oh no," replied Alice. "That would be absurd."

Another thump.

"Then what's that?" asked Marissa.

"I believe that's a pony," said Alice.

A severe-looking man in a black suit entered from the other side of the room. He had a thick black mustache that hung like a frown, and thinning black hair on his long, narrow head.

"Mr. Loeb!" Alice smiled. "So good to see you!"

"Miss Roosevelt," the man responded in a low, bored voice.

Then he noticed Marissa and Clara, and squinted at them through his spectacles. "And who do we have here," he said flatly.

"School chums of the children," Alice lied.

"Hmm," Mr. Loeb replied, eyeing the girls with suspicion. "I trust you'll behave yourselves while on White House grounds. Frankly, I'd prefer that you not sit on the furniture with those filthy clothes."

Marissa and Clara both looked down. In the sunlight, the dresses they'd found in the clubhouse looked much dustier than they'd seemed in the candlelight.

Mr. Loeb's eyes moved disapprovingly to their bare feet. He scowled at the sugar cubes on the floor, still lying where Clara had knocked them from the bowl.

"Sorry," Clara said, picking up the sugar cubes and tucking them into the sash of her fancy old dress.

There was another thump from the Red Room. Mr. Loeb glanced toward it, but Alice grabbed his arm and steered his attention back to her.

"Busy day?" Alice asked.

"Quite," said Mr. Loeb, retrieving a gold pocket watch from his vest. "I'm late to meet with the California delegation to discuss arrangements for your father's visit."

"We're from California!" said Clara.

"Grand," Mr. Loeb responded dryly.

"Ladies," Alice said, turning to the girls, "this is Mr. William Loeb, Father's private secretary. He's planning Father's little train adventure."

"Industry tour," said Mr. Loeb.

"Of course," said Alice. "All factories, no fun."

"The president himself set the agenda, Miss Roosevelt."

"Yes, my father has been a bit of a stick-in-the-mud lately," responded Alice, adjusting her white gloves. "Always talking about steel and mining and politics. Hardly gets outside into nature anymore—seems to have forgotten who he really is."

"I have no idea what you're on about, Miss Roosevelt," said Mr. Loeb.

"You wouldn't, would you," said Alice.

Then she saw something behind Mr. Loeb and her eyes widened. Marissa followed her gaze and saw a small brown pony with a long white mane, walking across the rug.

"Perhaps," said Alice, trying to keep Mr. Loeb from turning around, "the western air will do my father some good. He likes his birds and specimens so much more than he likes us, truth be told—you will let the president engage in a bit of bird-watching, won't you, Mr. Loeb?"

"Birds can't vote, Miss Roosevelt," said Mr. Loeb.

"And neither can women," replied Alice.

Quentin silently tiptoed into the room, trying to catch the pony.

"But surely," Alice quickly added, "you don't think that means that women don't matter, do you, Mr. Loeb?"

The pony stopped by a window. Quentin tried to hide it behind the green curtains.

"Of course women matter, Miss Roosevelt," he said, turning to look toward the window.

The pony's head stuck out between the curtains, but in a room full of animal heads, Mr. Loeb didn't notice it.

"Then I'm sure you'd agree," said Alice, bringing Mr. Loeb's eyes back to her, "that it would be helpful to have a woman's perspective on board for this trip, wouldn't you?"

"The first lady was invited," Mr. Loeb said. "She declined."

"Leaving an open space for the first daughter, no?" said Alice.

Behind Mr. Loeb, the pony was on the move again, sniffing the floor for food. It headed straight toward Clara. Clara moved away from Mr. Loeb and Alice, and the pony followed her. She moved faster, and so did the pony.

"Miss Roosevelt," said Mr. Loeb, "the president has already expressed his wish for the children to remain home."

The pony had huge teeth.

"I know what Father said," said Alice, "but couldn't you—"

"I don't create policy," said Mr. Loeb, "I enforce it."

Clara ran for the lobby and the pony trotted after her, its hooves rattling noisily against the marble floor.

"What on earth . . ." said Mr. Loeb, starting to turn around.

"Mr. Loeb!" Alice exclaimed brightly as she grabbed his arm and turned him back to face her. "If I can't visit California," she said, maintaining a commanding grip, "at least let me walk you to your California meeting."

As Alice led the confused man out through the Red Room, the pony chased Clara across the lobby. A Marine saluted. Clara ran into the East Room, where she liked to roller-skate. But now it was

hot, dark, and stank of sweat. On the far side of the room, deep in the shadows, two men were punching each other in the face.

Clara backed out of the room. The pony skidded past her, sliding into the East Room and turning sharply with a clatter of hooves to continue the chase back across the lobby floor.

"WHOOOAAAH!" Quentin yelled as he nearly crashed into Clara. He grabbed for the reins but missed as the pony's head dodged to the side, white mane sweeping through the air.

"WHAT IN THUNDERATION IS GOING ON OUT THERE?" one of the men in the East Room shouted.

"Run!" said Quentin.

Clara ran back across the lobby. The Marine saluted again. She saw a brightly lit doorway and ran through it, only to find herself trapped in a small elevator lined with mirrors and brass fixtures. Clara's reflection stared back at her from every angle.

The pony appeared in every mirror as well, its head right behind Clara, its teeth even larger in reflection. Clara backed up against the back wall as the pony lunged toward her.

"Father's new elevator!" said Quentin, squeezing in. "Great idea!"

"Get him away from me!" said Clara.

"Give him the sugar!" said Quentin.

Clara found the sugar cubes tucked in the sash of her dress. This was why the pony was chasing her. She winced as the grateful animal sloppily ate from her hand.

Then a voice shouted from across the lobby, "HOW is a man supposed to EXERCISE in this MADNESS?"

"Let's get out of here," Quentin whispered.

He slid the brass cage across the doorway and pulled the lever all the way over. The tiny elevator groaned and jolted upward.

Algonquin leaned in and breathed on Clara's hair.

"Horse slobber!" Clara whimpered.

"You don't like ponies?" said Quentin as the first floor slid down and the second floor came into view.

"I don't like animals," said Clara.

Quentin's hand slipped off the lever and the elevator stopped short, halfway between the first and second floors. He stared at Clara, shocked.

"And you call yourself a kid?" He shook his head and started the elevator again.

Back in the lobby, Marissa came out of the dining room just in time to see Clara's feet and Quentin's boots and Algonquin's hooves rise out of sight behind the brass cage.

"HALT!" shouted a man's voice.

Standing in the East Room doorway, scowling and breathing heavily, was a man wearing nothing but a pair of brown woolen shorts, leather shoes, and laced-up leather boxing gloves. His red hair was bushy and wild. His red mustache had a thin trickle of blood running down from his nose. His eyes burned as he stared right at her.

Marissa remembered those eyes, staring down from a painting. But this was no painting.

This was Theodore Roosevelt.

Roosevelt's eyes narrowed and his lips pulled back in a snarl as he took a step toward Marissa, pointing his boxing glove at her.

"Are you responsible for this madness?" he demanded.

Marissa had no words.

"Bad enough I have to let senators in my house," Roosevelt said, mopping the dust and sweat and blood from his face. He looked at the hoofprints on the lobby floor. His face turned a darker shade of red. "But I will NOT abide ENEMY CAVALRY rampaging through my CAMP!"

Marissa stood paralyzed, unable to speak, unable to move.

Something neighed upstairs.

Roosevelt's eyes looked upward. He ran to the main staircase and made it halfway up the stairs before a clattering noise made him leap out of the way. A blond girl in a purple dress slid down past him on a metal serving tray.

"Hi, Father!" the girl said as she skittered across the marble floor.

"Don't you 'Hi, Father' me, young lady," sputtered Roosevelt.

A second man emerged from the East Room, also wearing nothing but shorts, shoes, and boxing gloves. He looked like a giant, with long, muscular arms and a mustached face lined with the scars of a lifetime of punches.

"I didn't mean to get your nose, sir," said the giant.

"You caught a lucky break, Mr. Sullivan!" Roosevelt said, turning to face him. "I was DISTRACTED!"

The girl jumped up from her tray and grabbed Marissa's hand. "Follow me!" she said, tugging Marissa toward the dining room. The girl slid beneath the wooden eagle table and tapped the wing. The panel opened and the girl gripped the underside of the table, swinging herself into the tunnel feetfirst. Marissa did the same, flying down the slide much more gracefully than she had the first time.

"WHERE DID THOSE RAPSCALLIONS GO?" shouted Roosevelt, storming into the dining room and glaring around the empty room.

Hoofbeats echoed through the ceiling. Roosevelt turned and bounded up the stairs.

CHAPTER 4

SMOKE

"FATHER'S coming!" said Quentin as he stood on the second floor, desperately trying to yank Algonquin out of the elevator. The pony refused to budge, entranced by its own image in the mirrors of the elevator.

Clara tried to squeeze out of the elevator by climbing on the brass handrail. She slipped and fell onto the pony's back. The pony backed out of the elevator and bolted down the hallway, with Clara sprawled on its back.

Quentin sprinted down the hall and opened a door near the end. The pony galloped through and into a long bedroom. Quentin slammed the door shut.

Clara fell off the pony's back and flopped awkwardly onto the wooden floor. She got up and looked around. It was her bedroom. But instead of her bunkbed, it had two brass beds, side by side, and in one of them sat a sick-looking young boy in blue-and-white-striped pajamas.

"Algonquin!" the boy squealed in sleepy delight.

"That's Archie," said Quentin, locking the door. "He's got measles."

"I'm Clara. I got vaxxed."

Archie crawled out of bed and flung his arms around the pony's neck. "I missed you, pal!" he said, affectionately stroking the long white mane.

The door rattled. "Open up, you little vandals!" Roosevelt's voice commanded from the other side.

Archie and Quentin exchanged wide-eyed looks. Archie tossed a sheet over the pony. Quentin threw open the second-story window, climbed outside, and disappeared.

Roosevelt pounded his boxing-gloved fist against the door.

"Is that you, Father?" Archie said in a weak voice. "Mother said I mustn't get out of bed."

Archie looked at Clara and pointed at the window.

Clara leaned over the windowsill and saw the two-story drop to the lawn below. She saw a knotted rope connected to the window frame, leading to the nearby branch of a large maple tree. She put her hand on the rope. It felt flimsy. She looked back at Archie.

The door rattled again. "Someone open this confounded door!" yelled Roosevelt. "They give me a navy and an army, but not the keys to my own house!"

"What's the matter?" Archie whispered to Clara. "Can't climb trees?"

Clara glared at him, then lifted her legs over the window sash, grabbed onto the rope, and swung out. Her legs dangled over the fifteen-foot drop as she made her way, hand over hand, to the tree branch. She heard the window close behind her as she climbed onto the branch and crawled barefoot over to the sturdy trunk of the tree.

She saw Quentin running across the lawn below, with several rabbits hopping alongside him. There were other animals too. The South Lawn of the White House was more like a barnyard, with chickens and dogs wandering everywhere. A blue parrot flew by. She was about to climb down and follow Quentin, but she froze when she saw Mr. Loeb approaching. With him were two men in fancy coats. One was a short man with a white carnation in the lapel of his pinstriped suit. The second was an older man, with a top hat and a cane with a silver tip.

"Bird-watching, gentlemen," said Mr. Loeb as they stopped directly below the tree where Clara was sitting. "Alice wants him to go bird-watching."

"Presidents don't have time to watch birds!" exclaimed the old man with the cane.

"They don't have time to camp, either," grumbled Mr. Loeb, "but the little ones keep whining for that as well. I'm looking forward to getting him away from his children on this trip. They are terrible for his work ethic."

"If he wants to get out into the woods, bring him to my valley!" said the short man.

"I thought there were no woods left there, Wendell," said the old man.

"I've cut them all down except for one, Mr. Chairman," said Wendell.

"Ah yes," said the chairman, "the Steeple Giant. Quite the tourist attraction. I've received letters from citizens concerned about your little plan. Over a millennium old, isn't it? Older than King Arthur!"

"One millennium, two millennium, who knows," said Wendell.

"Two millenni-*ah*," corrected the chairman.

"Sure, make it *three* million!" said Wendell. "It's had a good run. But San Francisco needs electricity more than the forest needs another overgrown fern."

"We must have progress," sighed the chairman.

"Indeed we must," said Mr. Loeb. "I'll make sure the president understands."

"Much obliged, William," said Wendell. "Bring him by the site, we'll throw a grand ball for him on a stump! Here, let me show you what the *San Francisco Call* wrote about our last little party."

Wendell started digging through his briefcase, muttering to himself and making little distressed noises. "Hmm, I seem to have misplaced my newspaper."

"Pity," said Mr. Loeb in a bored voice.

"I brought it all the way east just to show it to the president!" exclaimed Wendell. "I knew he'd find it interesting. His boy certainly did."

"You showed the newspaper to one of the children?" asked Mr. Loeb.

"Why, yes," said Wendell, "the little boy saw me reading it in the Red Room, and he asked me if it had funny pages—and then I closed my eyes for a brief rest . . ."

"Yes, well," said Mr. Loeb dryly, "I can't possibly imagine what happened to your newspaper." He looked at his pocket watch. "But you'll have to excuse me, gentlemen, we have a train to catch."

"I'll see you on the train, William," Wendell replied.

Mr. Loeb walked away. Wendell produced a pair of cigars and handed one to the chairman. As he lit them both, a thick cloud of smoke rose up through the branches to Clara's hiding place. Her eyes watered and she felt a cough tickling its way up her throat.

"King Arthur?" said Wendell. "Really, Mr. Chairman?"

The chairman chuckled. "It is a fine old tree."

"And it'll make a lot of fine old parlor floors," replied Wendell. "Provided your committee doesn't stand in the way."

"That is valuable wood, isn't it?" asked the chairman. "I'm told only one in twenty of the old big trees still stand. They're headed the way of the dodo bird."

"Well, Mr. Chairman," responded Wendell, "stop by the mill after we shoot this particular dodo down. We'll cut you a round table, thirty feet across, so you can live like King Arthur."

Both men laughed, and continued puffing on their cigars. Clara fought the urge to gag as the smoke became thicker. Her neck was aching from sitting in the same position. Finally she couldn't hold it in any longer. She coughed.

"What was that?" Wendell said, squinting up into the tree. Clara pressed herself against the trunk, hoping to remain unseen.

Wendell shrieked and pointed at something on a lower branch. "A leopard!"

"Oh, don't be silly," said the chairman. "There couldn't be a—"

Then the chairman saw it and ran away. Wendell dropped his cigar in the dry grass and tripped over one of the tree roots, falling face first into the dirt. He stumbled away from the tree and ran across the lawn, arms flailing.

As Clara watched from above, a furry spotted animal leapt from the low branch of the tree. It looked up, with a face that seemed more like a dog's than a cat's. It made a hooting sound, as if it was laughing at her. The creature scampered after the men.

Clara smelled smoke. She looked down and saw Wendell's abandoned cigar, and the smoldering grass surrounding it. A breeze fanned the flames.

Clara looked out and saw Quentin on the hill, playing with the rabbits.

"Quentin!" she shouted, then coughed as the smoke surrounded her.

The fire below gathered strength and reached along the side of the trunk.

Clara held her breath and made her way down, branch by branch, until she was less than ten feet above the fire. She jumped and hit the ground several feet from the fire with a painful turn of her ankle. She stood up.

A blast of water knocked her down again.

"Sorry!" yelled Quentin as he tried to get control of the canvas garden hose in his hand.

Clara picked herself up from the muddy ground and hobbled over as Quentin lost his grip and the hose whipped wildly in the air, sending cascades of water everywhere except for the fire. Clara grabbed hold of the front, and she and Quentin turned the blast of water to the base of the tree. The flames hissed, then trickled away in a cloud of white steam.

"We did it!" yelled Quentin.

He turned back with a grin as the water continued soaking the charred roots of the tree. Clara limped over to the shed and turned off the hose.

"Did you see me?" exclaimed Quentin. "I was extraordinary!"

"Yeah," said Clara. "Extraordinary."

Then Clara was knocked to the ground again as something large slammed into the back of her legs. She landed with a splash on the muddy ground as a large white pig settled in alongside her, happily rolling around.

"That's Maude," said Quentin. "She's our pig."

"Of course she is," said Clara.

CHAPTER 5

THE MISSION

AT the bottom of the slide, Marissa watched through the clubhouse door as the blond girl in the purple dress lit candles.

"Thanks for the rescue," said Marissa. "How'd you know I was—"

"A White House kid?" asked the girl. "For one thing, your dress is twenty years behind the fashion, and you're wearing it backwards. Also, I overheard your entire conversation with Quentin and Alice. My bedroom is above the dining room."

"So is mine!" said Marissa.

"Intriguing," said the girl. "Well, you can't have it till I'm done with it. Oh, by the way, if you ever run into the Lincoln boys," she said, gesturing toward one of the cobwebbed doors, "tell them Ethel Roosevelt says hello, won't you?"

"Uh, yeah . . ." said Marissa. "Listen . . . Ethel . . . this is really cool, but how do we get back to our, you know, time?"

Ethel frowned. "Leaving so soon?"

"I think your dad would have me arrested if I went back there."

Ethel shook her head. "Father wears no spectacles when he's exercising. You're nothing but a blur to him."

She settled into an easy chair, resting her head on one of the arms and slinging her legs over the other. "But you're certainly welcome to hide out here." She picked up a book and started to read.

"Oh, now that I know there's a clubhouse in my basement," said Marissa, "I plan on hiding out here a lot. Like maybe the next four to eight years."

Ethel smiled sympathetically. "It doesn't work that way."

"What do you mean, 'It doesn't work that way'?"

"I mean just that. The clocks back in your time are stopped," said Ethel. "It'll all be waiting for you after your mission."

Marissa looked up. "What mission?"

Ethel closed her book and looked at Marissa with a single eyebrow raised. "You didn't think you could just hop around time like a tourist, did you? You've got work to do!"

"Now hold on a minute," said Marissa, "I didn't sign up for any—"

"Actually, you did," said Ethel, gesturing at the old parchment on the table across the room. "'We promise to help each other,' help the president, help the country and all that . . . You did sign, didn't you?"

"Yeah, but . . ." Marissa shook her head and slumped down on the couch. "That's not like a contract, is it? I mean, do we really have to complete a mission every time we go to the clubhouse?"

"Only when you leave through someone else's door." Ethel

paused. "You made a choice today, to come to our time instead of returning to your own."

"That was an accident!"

"Most of history is an accident," replied Ethel.

Marissa got up and tried one of the doors. It was locked. She tried another. Locked.

"Four months I've been trapped in *my* White House," Marissa said, "and when I finally find a way to break free, I'm trapped in *your* White House."

"Do you want to play poker?" asked Ethel as she walked over to a table full of games and picked up a deck of cards.

"No," said Marissa.

"I'm quite good. I can teach you," said Ethel. "Alice taught me."

"I don't want to play cards!" said Marissa, kicking one of the doors and badly stubbing her toe.

She hobbled back to one of the couches.

"I want to go home," she said, then added, "I mean, *real* home. Back to California. Away from the White House forever."

"The White House isn't so bad," said Ethel, eyeing pieces on a chessboard. "Think of it this way. Very few kids will ever get the chance that we have. Because of where we live and who we know, we can actually make things happen. Big things."

"Yeah, yeah," said Marissa, "it's an honor. So what big things do I have to do to get out of here? What's the mission?"

Ethel shrugged. "I don't know."

She returned to her chair and her book. "It'll present itself."

"Great," said Marissa, picking up a first edition of *Little Women* and flipping through its crisp white pages. "'It'll present itself.'"

Then Clara slid into the room.

"Marissa!" she exclaimed as she ran over and tried to give her sister a muddy, wet hug.

"What happened to you?" Marissa asked, fending her off.

"Everything!" said Clara. "But now I really have to shower. Mom will kill us if we're late for dinner."

"We're not late," said Marissa. "We're over a century early. And stuck that way."

Quentin rolled into the clubhouse with a big smile on his soot-covered face. "We saved a tree!" he yelled.

"Bully for you," mumbled Ethel, keeping her eyes on the page.

"It woulda burned down if it weren't for us!" Clara said.

"Probably the whole White House too!" said Quentin.

"Wait, you guys put out a fire?" asked Marissa.

She turned to Ethel. "Well, that's helping, isn't it? Was that the mission?"

Ethel looked up skeptically, then walked over to a door that had less cobwebs and dust than the others. She put her hand on the doorknob. She tried to turn it and shook her head.

Marissa ran over to the same door and tried it as well. The doorknob wouldn't move.

"Oh come on!" Marissa said, looking at the ceiling. "How much more help do you want?"

Ethel shrugged. "Maybe saving one tree isn't big enough."

Marissa stopped. One tree. "That's it!"

"What's it?"

"The tree's not big enough!" Marissa said slowly, her eyes widening. "We've got a bigger tree to save!"

Ethel shook her head. "I was not speaking in a literal manner . . ."

"Look at this!" said Marissa, pulling out the newspaper page in her pocket. She spread it out on a table and pointed at the photograph of the Steeple Giant and the dead valley surrounding it, with a dance party on one of the stumps.

"I've seen that guy!" said Clara, pointing to a small, oval-framed drawing near the base of the page. The drawing showed a man with a twirly mustache. The caption read: Arnold Wendell, chief financier, Wendell Dam. Clara told the others about the conversation she'd overheard while hiding in the tree.

Ethel rolled her eyes. "Frankly, I don't consider Mr. Loeb a good influence on Father."

"He said the same thing about you guys," said Clara. "Said you're terrible for your dad's work ethic."

"I'll show him terrible!" Ethel grumbled. "What kind of an idiot drops a lit cigar under a tree?"

"An adult," said Quentin.

"To be fair," said Clara, "he was being attacked by a leopard."

"Hyena," said Quentin. "That was a hyena."

"His name is Bill," explained Ethel.

"A hyena?" asked Marissa.

"Yeah, that's not a normal pet," said Clara.

"Work ethic," Ethel growled indignantly. "What do adults know about work ethic? Kids are the only ones who get anything done around here! Do they think Louisiana just purchased itself?"

"We're always cleaning up their messes," said Quentin.

"Like putting out that fire!" said Clara.

"Imagine the damage that Wendell fellow would have done if we hadn't been around to stop it!" said Quentin.

Marissa pounded her fist on the table and everybody went silent.

"We don't have to imagine," said Marissa. She pointed at the newspaper picture. "Look what he did already."

They all remained quiet for a moment, looking at the picture of empty stumps. And the last tree standing.

"Three hundred feet high," Ethel sighed as she read the article.

"That's a lie," said Quentin. "Father always said you shouldn't believe everything you read in the papers."

"But—" said Marissa.

"Three hundred feet tall," Quentin snorted. "That's as big as the Washington Monument. No tree is that big."

"How do you know?" said Clara.

"Because I've never seen a tree that was anywhere *near* three hundred feet. And I've seen a *lot* of trees."

"Have you ever been to California?" asked Clara.

"No . . ."

"So how can you be so sure?"

Quentin sniffed and walked over to the little table with all the wooden jigsaw puzzles and board games.

"All right," he said, "I'll go to California."

"No you won't," said Ethel.

Quentin stuck out his chin defiantly and announced, "I am going to see this tree for myself before they chop it down."

"And how do you plan on doing that?" asked Ethel.

"I'll sneak onto Father's train."

"That's nuts," said Clara.

"I did it before," said Quentin. "Me and Archie once hung onto the back of Father's carriage and rode all the way to—"

"The Capitol," said Ethel. "One mile from here. And you still got caught."

"I don't care," said Quentin. "I'm sneaking onto that train. I'm going to see that tree. And if it really is that big, I'm going to stop them from taking it down."

"All by yourself?" laughed Ethel.

"Yeah!" said Quentin. "I'll climb to the top and I won't let go!"

"No offense," said Clara, "but those trees are a lot taller than the one outside your window."

"No offense, but I'm still the best climber here," said Quentin.

"I bet I can climb better than you," said Clara.

"You?" Quentin said skeptically. "*You* were scared of a little pony!"

Quentin reached over to the chessboard and picked up a piece in the shape of a horse's head. He ran toward Clara shouting "Neigh! Neigh! Algonquin's coming to get you!"

"Stop it!" Clara squealed as she ran around the other side of the table, knocking over a stack of art supplies.

As Quentin ran by, Ethel grabbed the chess piece from his hand.

"That's my knight!" Ethel shouted. "Did you move anything else?" She ran over to the chessboard. "Where is the rook? I had Margaret Truman in check!"

As Ethel tried to restore the chessboard, Marissa looked again at the picture. She could hear the branches swaying. Creaking. Whispering. There was something about that tree.

"OK, Quentin," said Marissa, "let's figure out how to sneak you onto that train."

"Swell!" the boy exclaimed.

"You're not honestly going along with this madness, are you?" asked Ethel.

"We have to keep them from cutting the Steeple Giant down!" said Marissa, surprising herself with the level of passion in her voice.

"Maybe that's not your mission," said Ethel.

"Who cares!" Marissa responded. "Quentin's willing to do this, so we should help him!"

Ethel shook her head. "One tree?"

"It's not just one tree," said Marissa, "it's like . . . history, like an endangered species."

"Like the buffalo!" exclaimed Quentin. "Father saved the buffalo!"

"Father *helped* save the buffalo," corrected Ethel. "And that was before he was president. He doesn't care about such things anymore."

"Maybe Quentin can make him care," said Marissa. "Get him to go camping and, I don't know, find himself or something. You said he was always happiest—"

"You can't change the world with a camping trip," said Ethel. "All Quentin will do is annoy Father."

"And Mr. Loeb," said Quentin, playing with the tin soldiers on the floor. "I can really annoy Mr. Loeb."

Marissa heard a sound outside the doorway. "Someone's out there!"

"Impossible," said Ethel with a dismissive wave. "Just like this plan. Quentin lacks the maturity to pull it off."

"Oh and you think you could do it better?" asked Quentin.

"Of course," said Ethel. "I'm the responsible one. I'll go."

"No!" said Quentin. "This was *my* idea!"

"Why don't you both go?" asked Clara.

"No!" Ethel and Quentin answered at once.

"Whatever happened to . . ." said Marissa, walking over to the parchment and reading, "'we promise to help each other'?" She looked at Ethel and said, "You did sign this, didn't you?"

Ethel's eyes narrowed and her nose crinkled. "Fine," she said. "We'll all go."

"Well, not . . . all . . ." said Marissa, holding her hands up. "I mean, we're going to *help* you get on the train, but—"

"Oh no," said Ethel. "If we're doing something this stupid, you're coming with us."

"But—"

"Didn't you say you wanted to go back to California?" asked Ethel.

"That's not what I meant, and you know it," said Marissa.

"Scared to leave the White House?"

"No!"

"All that big talk about being trapped and breaking free and—"

"OK!" exclaimed Marissa. "I'm going!"

Ethel, Marissa, and Quentin all turned to Clara.

Clara looked back at all three, then stuck out her chin and shouted, "You're not gonna leave *me* behind!"

CHAPTER 6

THE LIGHT BRIGADE

AS the hour approached for President Roosevelt's departure, the White House became a flurry of activity. Trunks and bags were piled in the upstairs hallway, waiting to be taken down to the carts and wagons outside. Men in suits and women in long dresses scurried up and down the hall as porters hefted file cabinets, typewriters, trunks, and bags down the stairs.

Marissa huddled against the door inside Ethel's room, listening to the commotion in the hall. Clara twirled and watched the yellow folds flare out on the frilly dress she'd borrowed from Ethel. Marissa fidgeted and tugged at the long sleeves of the borrowed pink dress she now wore. The lacy collar was choking her all the way up to her chin.

Ethel was packing every piece of clothing she owned in order to dress all three girls on the trip. She had the clothes divided into two large trunks, leaving room in each one.

"You've got a lot of pretty dresses," Clara observed.

"Not as many as Princess Alice," Ethel said sarcastically.

"Do you think we should tell her our plan?" asked Marissa.

"Alice?" said Ethel. "Heavens, no! She'd never allow it."

"But she's a White House kid too, isn't she?" asked Marissa.

"Barely. More of a White House adult really," said Ethel. "I don't know why she lives here anymore. Always fighting with Mother. Rarely speaks with Father."

"Alrighty then," said Marissa, realizing she'd brought up a sore subject. She cracked open the door and peeked into the hallway. "Here comes Quentin."

"Finally," Ethel muttered.

Quentin entered the room with a stick over his shoulder. Tied to the stick was a cloth bundle and a pair of boots. He dropped the stick into the corner.

"You couldn't find a suitcase?" asked Ethel.

"We're sneaking onto a train," Quentin explained impatiently. "This is how you carry your stuff when you sneak onto a train."

"This isn't the funny pages, Quentin!" said Ethel. She looked at the small bundle. "You know we're leaving for several weeks, right?"

"I brought extra socks," said Quentin.

Ethel rolled her eyes and gestured toward one of the trunks. Quentin threw his stick, boots, and bundle inside, and Ethel tucked it in among her dresses before closing the lid. She took one last look around the room and closed the other trunk as well.

"OK. I think we're ready," said Ethel.

"Does Archie know his part?" asked Marissa.

Quentin nodded. "He'll be listening for the secret code."

"You couldn't just knock on his door?" asked Clara.

"Everybody shush," said Marissa as she cracked the door open once more. The hallway was crowded and busy. "OK, guys," Marissa said, "you're on!"

Quentin and Ethel ran out of the room toward the men handling the luggage.

"I want to help!" Quentin yelled cheerfully. He grabbed a tall stack of papers and started weaving his way toward the stairs, pages fluttering off the top. Several of the adults trailed him nervously, picking up pages along the way.

Ethel grabbed a cart piled high with three trunks and pushed it as hard as she could toward the elevator at the end of the hall. "I'm helping too!" she called out as the rest of the adults in the hall ran after her and the swaying tower of luggage.

With everyone in the hall distracted, Marissa and Clara lugged the first trunk out of Ethel's room and slid it in among the others lining the wall. As Quentin ran into a light fixture, his stack of paper collapsed into a thousand floating pages. Marissa and Clara carried out the second trunk and shoved it next to the first. Marissa opened the lid and jumped inside, pushing aside the dresses to make room. Clara climbed in after her and pulled the lid closed.

Marissa and Clara huddled silently in their trunk as they listened to the grown-ups in the hall politely urging Quentin and Ethel to stop "helping." Marissa cracked open the trunk lid and saw Quentin standing in the middle of a blizzard of flying paper.

Quentin leaned back, cupped his mouth with his hands, and yelled, "Half a league! Half a league! Half a league onward!"

A door flew open, and out galloped Algonquin with Archie on its back, still in blue pajamas, wearing a metal pot on his head and pointing a broomstick like a lance.

"Forward, the Light Brigade!" the boy shouted as they galloped through the adults in the hall, sending another burst of paper into the air. "Charge for the guns!"

The adults scattered in panic, stampeding over each other to get to the stairs as Archie wheeled Algonquin around for another pass. In the chaos, no one noticed as Quentin and Ethel hid themselves in the other trunk.

When the hallway had cleared, Archie dismounted Algonquin and pushed down on the lids of both trunks. "Have a nice trip, rascals," he said. "You'd better bring me back a good souvenir."

"Loeb!" yelled a voice from beyond the double doors at the end of the hall.

Archie looked up in panic and sprinted into his room, leaving the pony behind. A moment later, the double doors at the end of the hall burst open and President Roosevelt marched out of his office, dressed in a black suit. He frowned at the papers scattered around the hallway. Then he noticed Algonquin. He took a step closer to the pony, his fists tightening.

Roosevelt's face darkened to a deep red, rivaling the color of his hair and mustache. His breathing became louder, coming out of him in great heaves. His lips pulled back into a wild snarl that showed every one of his gritted teeth. His eyes tightened to narrow squints.

He began to shake. Then he began to laugh.

Mr. Loeb came running up the stairs. Roosevelt saw him and laughed even harder, gasping as he tried to regain control, pointing at the animal.

Finally Roosevelt managed to choke out, "Loeb! My children are an industrious lot, are they not? How do you suppose they got this beast up the stairs?"

"Perhaps . . . the elevator?" said Mr. Loeb.

Roosevelt grinned and said, "I knew these modern conveniences would come in handy! Creative thinking there, Loeb. I suppose you'll have to use the same method to get him down."

Mr. Loeb's shoulders sagged. "Me . . . sir?"

"You're the only man I trust with this mission," said Roosevelt, releasing the pony's neck and placing the reins in Mr. Loeb's hands.

"Now," Roosevelt said with a pleasant grin, "get this mule out of the house before Edith sees it, or we'll all wind up in the stockade!"

Roosevelt strode down the hall, right past the trunks where the children were hiding. He called over his shoulder, "And when you're done with that, Mr. Loeb, let's saddle up and head west. Lock and load!"

Mr. Loeb summoned a staff member up the stairs and handed off the reins. Soon the pony was gone, and the hallway flooded with activity again as staffers scrambled to clean up the scattered papers.

Marissa heard footsteps running in every direction and the sound of trunks and bags being moved. Her trunk jolted upward and crashed back down.

"Help me out," said a voice. "There must be cannonballs in here."

"Moose hunting," said another.

The trunk was unevenly hoisted from both ends, then dropped heavily on a rolling cart. The girls felt themselves being wheeled slowly into the elevator, which still smelled of pony. They were wheeled outside and roughly tossed onto a wagon. Marissa peeked from under the lid and saw the other trunk being loaded next to them.

Marissa heard a muffled sneeze, followed by Ethel's voice hissing "Quiet!"

The wagon lurched forward and began bouncing and jerking to the sharp clatter of hoofbeats. The uneven ride made Clara feel sick, but Marissa felt only excitement. She was finally leaving the White House.

Marissa cracked open the lid and looked out at the busy street. Bright storefronts and awnings flowed into view, along with dozens of people strolling the sidewalks.

Feathers stretched from the hats of elegant ladies. Young boys in flat wool caps jostled with each other to sell newspapers on street corners. Horses and carriages and streetcars and bicycles fought over the cobblestones of Pennsylvania Avenue. Then the noise of hoofbeats and carriage wheels was overtaken by the roar of an engine. A red-and-gold motorcar sped into view, sputtering fumes in every direction.

The car was close enough now that Marissa could hear the chugging pistons beneath its shiny red hood. The driver wore a brown hat and driving goggles. One leather-gloved hand furiously worked the levers and knobs while the other steered the big wheel. The driver leaned forward aggressively as the car closed to within a few feet of the wagon. The driver grinned, and looked straight at Marissa.

Marissa gasped and yanked the lid down. She sat frozen in the dark as she heard the motorcar roar past. The wagon jostled and bounced for several more minutes until it finally slowed. Workers roughly hoisted and dropped Marissa's trunk, sending a painful jolt up her spine.

Marissa cracked the lid again. The other trunk was piled next to hers among many other pieces of luggage. Beyond the bags was a huge iron wheel. Lifting the lid of the trunk just a bit more,

Marissa saw she was next to a short passenger train, covered in red, white, and blue.

On the other side of the platform was a dirt parking lot, filled with carts and wagons of every shape and size. Parked among them was the red-and-gold motorcar. Marissa saw the young driver slip onto the train.

"All aboard the Presidential Special!" yelled a conductor. "Authorized passengers only!"

A serious-looking man wearing a bowler hat started down the platform, glaring in every direction. He turned and waved. A door from the station opened and President Roosevelt emerged, wearing a formal suit, a black overcoat, and a top hat. He shook hands with a few smiling railroad workers and leapt up the steps into a fancy burgundy car near the end of the train.

Marissa let the lid fall shut and waited. Soon she and Clara were floating through the air once again, being carried onto the train and tossed onto a hard metal surface. Something big and heavy was tossed on top of the trunk. There was a piercing whistle and the sound of another blast of steam. The train heaved forward, and the trunk began to sway. Slowly the train gathered momentum, rocking faster and faster, back and forth.

Marissa tried to push the lid open, but the heavy item on top of them prevented her from doing so. Air and light flowed in from a crack to the side, and the clacking of the wheels made Marissa feel drowsy. She leaned her head against the smooth fabric of one of Ethel's dresses.

As the president's train rolled westward, she drifted off to sleep.

CHAPTER 7

THE PRESS CAR

SOMETHING growled.

Clara's eyes opened. She saw nothing but dark.

The growl was close. Choking. Sputtering. Then silent.

Clara held her breath and listened. She heard the clatter of wheels below her. And the growl above her.

Clara tried to remain calm. She thought through everything she knew about the situation. She was in a trunk. She was in a trunk on a train.

The growl grew louder. Choking again. Sputtering again.

Clara knew she was on the train of a president who had many strange and dangerous pets, who'd probably come along for the ride and were now getting very hungry and looking for breakfast.

It growled again. Right above her. Clara wanted to scream.

She heard a voice. Also right above her.

"Quentin!" the voice said. It sounded like Ethel.

The growling stopped. "Wha?" said Quentin's sleepy voice.

"You were snoring!" said Ethel.

Clara let out a small giggle of relief.

There was a rustling sound above.

"Is that you, Clara?" Quentin's voice called down through the lid of the trunk.

"Yeah," she answered.

"We're stuck in here," said Quentin. "Help us get out!"

"How are we supposed to do that when your trunk is on our trunk?" Clara said.

"Our trunk won't open!" yelled Ethel's voice. "We must be buried in a pile of luggage."

"Buried alive!" said Quentin.

The rattling rhythm of the train's wheels continued below. Clara knocked on the walls of the trunk. On the left it sounded solid. On the right it was hollow.

"I don't think we're buried. We must be on a rack or something," said Clara. "Maybe we could fall off. Everybody lean to the right."

Ethel's voice said, "No, Quentin! That's your left."

Clara felt the rocking of the train car. "We just have to time it right," she said. "OK. Right!" Everyone leaned right. "Left!" Everyone leaned left. "Right! Left! Right! Left!" With every rock of the train, the swaying trunks seemed to lean out farther.

The train shook and the entire stack of luggage went tumbling. Clara crashed into Marissa as their trunk tumbled over and over until it landed hard on its side. They shoved the trunk lid open, got out, and stretched. The pale light of dawn filtered in from vents at the top of the metal walls on either side of the crowded baggage car.

The train slowed to a stop. Through the walls they could hear hundreds of voices cheering and chanting "Teddy!" over the sound of a marching band.

Clara and Marissa rolled the other trunk upright and lifted the lid. Quentin and Ethel climbed out, struggling to unwind their cramped limbs and rolling around their necks.

"What a ride," Quentin groaned. Then his face brightened. "Let's eat."

He reached back into the trunk and retrieved the stick with the bundle tied at the end. He untied the handkerchief to reveal four pairs of socks and a paper package containing a loaf of bread, four apples, a block of cheese, and a chunk of ham. He took out a pocketknife and began slicing pieces of cheese and ham on the lid of the trunk.

Clara hungrily took several pieces. Marissa looked at the food skeptically, then took an apple. Quentin held out a piece of cheese to Ethel, who rolled her eyes and said, "No thanks."

"What?" said Quentin with a mouth full of ham. "It's straight from the White House kitchen."

"I'd rather see what I can find in the dining car," Ethel responded.

"It's that way," Quentin said, pointing to the large metal door at the end of the baggage car. "You have to go through the press car first. Then it's the dining car. After that, the important people car."

"And how do you know that?" asked Ethel.

Quentin shrugged. "I reconnoitered."

"Reckon what?" asked Clara.

"I reconnoitered, it means looked around," said Quentin. "Father says a real soldier always reconnoiters before an operation."

"Oh and you're definitely a *real* soldier," muttered Ethel.

"I peeked out the trunk and watched the shoes when we were on the platform," Quentin continued, ignoring his sister. "Plain brown shoes got on the first car, white shoes on the next, and shiny black ones on the car after that."

The train jolted forward and the journey resumed.

"That was short," said Marissa.

"Just a whistle stop," said Quentin. "Long enough to take on water, exchange the mail, and let Father deliver a speech from the back." He sat back and added confidently, "It's standard procedure."

"Standard procedure," said Ethel sarcastically. "OK, train expert, let's see if you're right about the dining car next door."

"Not right next door, after the press car," Quentin said.

"OK," Ethel said as she climbed up another pile of luggage and made her way toward the end of the car.

Marissa got up. She looked back at Clara.

"I'm staying here," said Clara, grabbing another piece of cheese.

"Mph roo," said Quentin with a full mouth of ham.

"OK then," said Marissa, and she followed Ethel to the end of the car.

The metal sliding door was held in place by a black iron lever. As they walked toward it, the lever swung over on its own. The door began to slide open.

"*Hide!*" Ethel hissed. A fierce and dusty wind swept into the car.

A nervous-looking man in a red porter's uniform stepped inside.

"I'm sure of it, sir," the man shouted back over his shoulder. "Someone's in here!"

"Nonsense," replied a familiar low voice.

Mr. Loeb walked into the car. He scowled at the messy conditions in the baggage car, then looked over his shoulder and called, "Mr. Pinkerton!"

A third man entered, wearing a bowler hat. He had a tightly trimmed mustache.

Mr. Loeb turned to the man and said, "You swept this car thoroughly before we arrived, did you not?"

"Yes, sir," Pinkerton replied, striding confidently into the baggage car. "Nothing ever gets by us."

Ethel slipped by Pinkerton and ducked outside. Marissa followed her. Cold air smacked her face as she walked out onto the narrow ledge between train cars. Her ears filled with the pounding rhythm of the wheels. She saw Ethel disappear into the next car. There were no guardrails or chains spanning the gap. She bit her lip and took a big step across. She grabbed the door to the passenger car, yanked it open, and ducked inside.

The narrow wooden corridor that stretched before her was lined with windows on one side and passenger compartments on the other. Every compartment was closed. Marissa grabbed the handle of the nearest passenger compartment and ducked inside. She closed the compartment door behind her just as the voices of Mr. Loeb and the other men entered the corridor.

Marissa turned and was startled to see the young motorcar driver sitting on one of the cushioned benches. The driver was still wearing leather driving gloves and a brown hat pulled low over the eyes.

"Oh," said Marissa. "Hello."

The young driver looked away to the window without speaking.

"That one doesn't talk much," said a tall man sitting by himself on the other side of the compartment. He had light brown skin and wore a linen suit covered in the pattern of a grid.

"Gordon LePont," the man said, extending his hand to shake Marissa's. Then he reached into the pocket of his starched blue shirt and produced a business card between his index and middle fingers. He handed it to Marissa. "*San Francisco Call.*"

Marissa took the card and read the fancy writing identifying Gordon as a reporter.

"Family?" asked Gordon.

"What?"

"I assume you're somebody's family, yes?" said Gordon. "That's how you got on here?"

"Oh," said Marissa. "Right." It was true, in a way.

"Daughter to one of the senators, I expect?"

"Yes," she lied, hoping he wouldn't ask any more questions.

Gordon nodded, apparently satisfied.

He pointed at the young driver. "That one is Alex Lee. Writes for some paper out of the Midwest. That's about all I managed to get outta him. Though he managed to get a week's pay out of me playing cards last night."

Marissa sat down next to Alex Lee, accidentally knocking over a brown leather bag leaning against the bench. A small toy horse with a black triangle on its flank fell out of the bag. Alex Lee stuffed it back into the bag and went back to reading a large clothbound book. *Hunting Trips of a Ranchman*, by Theodore Roosevelt.

Outside the window, a barren valley came into view. The whistle blew and the brakes squealed. The train slowed and rumbled past hundreds of open bucket-shaped cars sitting on the next track, each filled with large chunks of black coal. Beyond the tracks were gray mountainsides, punctuated by black seams and pits.

There was a distant explosion, and a black cloud rose up from the ridgeline. Then another blast, followed by a low rumble, and the entire side of a mountain seemed to slide away in a billowing cloud of dust.

"That, my friends, is your new century," said a loud voice in the next compartment.

Gordon rolled his eyes and muttered, "Wendell."

Marissa recognized the name. It was the man Clara had spied on from her tree, the man whose picture had been in the paper next to all of those dead stumps.

"Arnold Wendell?" she asked. "The businessman?"

Gordon shrugged. "Businessman, oilman, timber man, however he describes himself this week. Got his hand in the pocket of every business trust and shady combination there is. I covered one of his silly parties in the woods—"

"That was you!" Marissa exclaimed.

"Beg pardon?"

"You wrote about the dance on the stump!"

Gordon looked at her with a wry smile. "You actually *read* that waste of ink?"

Through the wall, Wendell shouted, "God has blessed this nation with the resources to achieve greatness. We must rip these mountains asunder!"

Gordon shook his head. "Wendell's vocabulary gets prettier when he smells money. And if there's a dime in the ground, he'll quite literally move mountains to get it."

The train began winding along the curves of a slow brown river. The remains of choking mudslides streaked the treeless mountain on the other side. A long trickle of rust seeped from an exposed hillside.

"There, gentlemen," yelled Wendell, "a seam of iron! The very mountains are melting away and handing over their treasure to fuel the American destiny. Do we have the will to take it?"

"Take what?" another man's voice growled impatiently through the wall.

"The stuff of empire!"

"Enough stuff," the voice responded. "You gonna play cards?"

A raft of dead fish floated by on the river, their white underbellies gleaming in the sunlight. Farther upstream, a greasy black field appeared at the water's edge, with a handful of large, oil-pumping derricks slowly nodding up and down, spraying petroleum with every pull and dribbling rainbow-colored slicks into the water.

The train rounded a bend and rolled into a narrow canyon, its steep walls covered in lush green forest. Marissa was relieved to see something living after all of the bleak miles they'd traveled. A flock of birds rose from the treetops, and several deer ran from the forest into the steep open hillside. A mist was rising among the tall pine trees.

But as the train reached the edge of the forest, the mist thickened into smoke. Bright patches of flame appeared along the edge of the forest.

"Seriously?" Marissa asked under her breath.

"Pardon?" asked Gordon.

"Nothing," Marissa replied.

Gordon leaned over to the window and followed her gaze to the flames. "Oh, don't worry about that," he said. "It's a controlled burn. They're just clearing the land."

"I know," Marissa said, annoyed.

Gordon backed away with his hands up in mock surrender, an indulgent smile on his face. "OK, OK," he said.

"Sorry," said Marissa, "just, I mean . . . they couldn't leave . . . something?"

Gordon laughed and shook his head. "Kids."

He stood up in the swaying compartment and said, "Come on, let me introduce you to the distinguished gentlemen of the press."

Gordon led Marissa into the next compartment. It was packed. A sleeping rack near the ceiling hung open with a snoring man on top, one leg swaying over the edge with a brown shoe on it. Below the rack was a small table, with poker players squeezed tightly around it.

Most of the players were reporters like Gordon, but one of the men wore a much fancier suit, with a white carnation in the lapel. Marissa recognized him from the newspaper drawing as Arnold Wendell. He had a large stack of money in front of him.

But an even bigger stack, the largest on the table, was in front of the smallest player, casually chewing on a lollipop. Ethel.

"Oh no," said one of the players as he noticed Marissa, "not another little girl." He gestured at Ethel and said, "This hooligan already took our lunch money."

Gordon laughed and said, "Burns, if she's robbing from you, she's all right with me."

He gestured toward Marissa and said, "This one is the daughter of Senator, uh . . ."

"Delightful!" said Ethel, jumping up from the table and extending her hand to Marissa. "I'm Congressman Smith's daughter."

Marissa was shocked that a compartment full of reporters didn't seem to recognize Ethel as the president's daughter. Must be nice to live before the internet.

"I think we'll be great chums, don't you?" asked Ethel. She reached over to a tray of sandwiches and shoved one into Marissa's hand.

The brakes squealed and the train began to slow. Most of the men jumped up and tucked their reporter's notebooks into their jackets.

"Pittsburgh!" the conductor called out in the corridor.

The snoring man in the upper bunk awoke with a start, his brown shoe nearly kicking Wendell in the face.

"Pittsburgh?" the man asked. "What happened to Harrisburg?"

"You slept through it, Clement," said a reporter with a deeply curled mustache.

"Aw, Phillips," Clement protested, "you were supposed to wake me up!"

"Don't worry," said Phillips, pulling at the curled end of his mustache. "Teddy'll say the same thing here that he said back there."

"'I want to congratulate the farmers on their abundant crops of corn—'" said Gordon in a raspy imitation of President Roosevelt.

"'—and on their abundant crops of children,'" Burns finished for him. The train whistled and the brakes squealed. "Might as well get to it, boys."

The platform that rolled into sight outside the window was packed with men, women, and children dressed in their Sunday best, straining for a glimpse of the president. There was red-white-and-blue bunting everywhere, and American flags waving in every hand.

Phillips, Gordon, Burns, and Wendell made their way out of the compartment. Clement dropped down from the bunk and rubbed his eyes. He looked in confusion at the two girls for a moment, then shook his head and hurried down the corridor.

Ethel scooped her winnings into the fold of her skirt.

"You have to teach me how to play poker," said Marissa.

"I already offered, in the clubhouse," said Ethel. "Remember?"

"I was kinda busy," said Marissa.

"Yes, as I recall, you were kicking doors."

Ethel and Marissa grabbed the remaining sandwiches from the tray and hurried back up the empty corridor, out of the press car and back into the baggage car.

"Hey, Quentin, you were right about the press car," Ethel called out to the pile of luggage.

No one answered.

CHAPTER 8

PINKERTON

"QUENTIN?" Ethel called.

"Clara!" shouted Marissa.

Marissa scrambled over the chaotic piles of trunks and bags. She found Ethel's clothes scattered where they had fallen, but there was no sign of Clara or Quentin.

The silence in the car was shattered by the piercing whistle of the train. A loud burst of steam shook the car. The whistle blew again. And again. The train started to move.

Several children ran alongside, trying to keep pace with the president's train.

Marissa scanned the platform, desperate for some sign of her sister. The platform fell away as the train rolled on, past a lumber mill with workers standing on piles of cut logs, waving their hats. Women waved handkerchiefs from the windows of a redbrick factory building. The windows flew past, quicker and quicker, until the people inside were a blur and the bricks joined together in long red lines as the whistle continued to blow.

Marissa made her way down the swaying corridor of the press car, peeking into the compartments as she searched for her sister. As she reached the end of the car, she ran into Alex Lee, still wearing the brown hat, eyes widening at the sight of Marissa.

"Careful," the reporter whispered while walking past.

Marissa continued to the dining car. Electric bulbs glowed beneath polished brass fixtures. Clouds of fragrant steam rose from trays of beef, pork, chicken, mashed potatoes, and other vegetables. At the end of the table was a mountain of chocolate, with endless rows of cupcakes.

At a table halfway down the car, Mr. Loeb was dining with Wendell. Marissa ducked under the buffet table to avoid being seen. She crawled forward, trying to keep her stomach from growling from all of the wonderful smells drifting down from above.

Stay focused, she told herself. Find Clara. Ignore the cake.

She heard Wendell talking to Loeb.

"I don't like it, William!"

"Calm yourself, Arnold," replied Mr. Loeb's flat voice. "Try the oysters."

"Teddy is getting squishy!" Wendell whined in response. "He's reverting to nature boy."

"You will address him as President Roosevelt," Mr. Loeb responded with a slight edge of irritation. Then, in a quieter voice, "At least in public, Arnold. Show some respect."

"If he wants to stay president, he needs to respect California's delegates," warned Wendell.

"I'm well aware—"

"And if he wants California's delegates, he has to help clear the way for progress! Electricity! Industry! Dam the Sierras!"

"The president will agree," said Mr. Loeb. "I'll see to it."

"The nation's future depends on it!"

"Noted," Mr. Loeb responded dryly.

"Nature has blessed this nation with the resources to dominate the world!" said Wendell.

"So you've stated," said Mr. Loeb. "And if you listen to the president's speech when we arrive in Youngstown, I believe you'll see I have him well under control."

"Waiter!" a voice yelled. "Tray for the president!"

Marissa saw a pair of white shoes hurry up the aisle. As everyone in the car looked towards the president's tray, Marissa crawled to the end of the dining car and slipped out the door, crossing to the first-class car.

"Can you hold that for me, please?" said the waiter, balancing the president's silver domed tray.

Marissa nodded and held the door open.

The waiter smiled back and said "thank you very much" as he glided into the rich mahogany corridor with the practiced grace of a professional, and made his way down the plush red carpet. Marissa followed close behind, looking at the closed compartment doors, wondering if her sister was on this car.

"YOUNGS-town!" yelled a voice that made Marissa jump. From the far end of the car came a conductor with a walrus mustache. "YOUNGS-town, O-HI-o!" he cried.

Marissa opened the door for the waiter at the other end of the car, and followed him outside to the gap between the first-class car and the president's car.

An iron bench sat on the large deck beside the sliding door. The waiter set the president's silver domed tray on the bench. He gave three sharp knocks on the door, and without waiting for an answer, quickly headed past Marissa.

Marissa looked back at the president's door. It slid halfway open. Two large hands appeared and took the tray inside. The door slid shut.

"What are you doing here?" asked a sharp voice behind Marissa. She spun around to see Pinkerton, staring down at her under the rim of his bowler hat.

Before she could answer, the train whistle blew. The brakes squealed and the train seized up, throwing both Marissa and Pinkerton off balance. Pinkerton lunged toward her, and she ran under his arm and down the corridor.

"GET BACK HERE THIS INSTANT!" yelled Pinkerton.

The narrow corridor began to fill as first-class passengers emerged from their compartments for the next whistle stop. Marissa pushed forward through the men and women in fur coats and suit jackets as Pinkerton yelled, "STOP THAT GIRL!"

Marissa reached the end and burst into the dining car. She nearly collided with the waiter, who was carrying a large tray of silverware. He smiled at her, but the smile faded as the door behind Marissa flew open and Pinkerton rushed into the diner, cheeks flushed in rage, his bowler hat barely hanging on and his mustache a tortured mess.

Outside, the train crawled into the station for Youngstown, Ohio. A band was playing. The crowd was cheering. Flags were waving and the sun was shining.

"You!" yelled Pinkerton, pointing an accusing finger at Marissa. "Get back here!"

Marissa gave the waiter a pleading look. He gave her a quick nod. As Marissa hurried up the aisle, she heard a shattering crash behind her. She turned and saw the waiter and Pinkerton, tangled up amid a sea of forks, knives, and spoons that had scattered throughout the aisle.

"I'm so sorry, sir," Marissa heard the waiter say.

"Out of my way!" squealed Pinkerton, choking in anger.

"Of course, sir," said the waiter. "Just as soon as I pick up every one of these and put them in their proper place."

Marissa ran out of the diner car and into a pack of reporters, all pushing and shoving their way out of the press car and onto the station platform. Marissa merged into the center of the pack as the reporters hurried down the length of the train to join the many people gathered on the tracks behind the large metal deck on the caboose.

The deck was draped with red-white-and-blue banners and American flags. Surrounding the deck was a low iron fence with the presidential seal in the center. Several men were standing on the deck looking out over the crowd. One of them was Arnold Wendell, grinning. Next to him was Mr. Loeb, frowning.

Marissa slunk lower in the packed crowd, hiding beneath the dense canopy of women's church hats and men's straw boaters. The door to the caboose opened. The crowd surged in anticipation. The ground seemed to shake with an excited roar as President Roosevelt emerged, smiling wide and wiping his hands on a cloth napkin. He held his hands out for calm, but the crowd continued to cheer for several more minutes.

The train whistle blew, interrupting the crowd's cheering long enough for the president to shout, "Land sakes, Youngstown, let a man speak before they drag me off to Chicago!"

The crowd laughed and applauded.

"I apologize for my tardiness," shouted President Roosevelt, wiping his hands once more and touching his napkin to the corners of his mouth, "but I was just finishing off an Ohio chicken. My compliments to the farmer who produced that magnificent bird!"

The crowd laughed in appreciation.

"For that matter," Roosevelt added, "I'd like to compliment all the farmers here for their abundant crops of corn, and their abundant crops of children!"

Marissa saw the reporters exchange looks as they scribbled in their little notebooks.

"But I know this isn't just a farm city," said Roosevelt, "it's a steel town!"

The crowd cheered and pressed forward, pushing Marissa with it until she was right up against the deck where Roosevelt was shouting, "American steel will build American ships to proclaim the American empire!"

Marissa had a hard time breathing as the excited crowd pressed in even tighter.

"Nature has blessed this nation," shouted Roosevelt, "with the resources to dominate the world!"

Marissa looked up. Those were the very words Wendell had used before. She saw the businessman smiling appreciatively at Mr. Loeb.

"The stuff of empire!" cried Roosevelt. "Do we have the will to take it?"

The crowd shouted "Yes!"

The door behind the president burst open and Pinkerton stumbled out onto the deck, his eyes wild and angry. His hand shook, tightly clutching a large silver spoon.

Marissa ducked down between a woman in a wide skirt and a man in an army overcoat. Pinkerton shoved his way to the front of the speaking deck and stood right next to the president, who continued speaking about iron and coal. Mr. Loeb put a hand on Pinkerton's shoulder to pull him back, but Pinkerton shook him off, staring intently into the crowd. Pinkerton locked eyes with Marissa. His eyebrows lowered and he burst forward, vaulting past the president, over the railing, and into the surprised crowd.

Marissa tried to push her way back to the reporters but instead fell to the ground between the tracks. Her knee hit the sharp gravel and she winced in pain. She tried to move to her left, then her right, but she was hemmed in on both sides by adult legs jostling in confusion.

"Where is she?" demanded Pinkerton.

Marissa could see only one way out. Straight ahead. Underneath the train.

"Now, now, folks, just a little excitement," President Roosevelt said from above the metal deck as Marissa crawled under the caboose.

Marissa scurried forward toward the shaft of light where the caboose ended and the next car began. A whistle blew. Marissa crawled faster, splinters from the wooden railroad ties digging into her knees. She found an open spot between the wheels and scrambled out onto the side of the tracks. There were kids on this side of the tracks, dressed in shabby clothes, gathering coal from the tracks.

"STOP!" a voice behind her yelled.

Marissa looked over her shoulder and saw Pinkerton shove his way past one of the kids. The other kids pelted him with lumps of coal, giving Marissa a chance to run toward the front of the train. The whistle blew again, and the train began to roll.

"I SAID STOP!"

Marissa didn't look back. She kept running, her footsteps pounding on the loose gravel alongside the slowly accelerating train cars as she looked for a way back on board.

"Marissa!" shouted a voice from the front of the train.

Her chest hurting from exhaustion, her eyes stinging from the smoke, Marissa ran toward the voice. There was a bridge up ahead. She was about to run out of room. Then she saw Quentin, waving at her from atop the full coal car behind the locomotive.

"JUMP!" yelled a voice right beside Marissa. She turned her head and saw a metal ladder on the side of the baggage car. Marissa jumped for the ladder. One hand reached a metal rung but the other missed. Then somebody caught Marissa's other wrist and pulled her to safety. Marissa looked to see who had saved her.

There she was. Hair whipping wildly beneath an oversized engineer's cap. Soot covering the familiar dimples. Hand still gripping her sister's wrist.

"Clara!"

CHAPTER 9

THE COFFEEPOT

"HOW . . ." Marissa yelled, clutching the ladder tight enough to turn her knuckles white.

"I CAN'T HEAR YOU!" shouted Clara over the roar of the locomotive.

The train was now moving too fast for the girls to move off the ladder, so they hung on, side by side, as the train rolled through the vast cornfields of Ohio. Marissa's shoulders ached with the strain of holding on as the sun sank lower in the wide midwestern sky. After several hours, a town finally appeared on the horizon.

The whistle blew and the train slowed. Over the sound of squealing brakes, Marissa heard another band playing and another crowd cheering the approach of Teddy Roosevelt.

As the train rolled into the station, Clara stepped gracefully onto the front ledge of the baggage car. Marissa stiffly followed her after the train had lurched to a complete stop.

"OK!" said Marissa. "How did you get here?"

Clara pointed at a small door on the front of the baggage car.

"While you guys slipped out the big door in the back," said Clara, "me and Quentin found a way out the front."

"OK, but then—"

"Then we just walked across here . . ." Clara stepped on the iron peg joining the coal car to the baggage car and skipped across the gap, hoisting herself over the metal side of the coal car.

"That was swell!" yelled Quentin from the other side of the coal pile. "Did you see me? I didn't get scared or anything!"

Clara rolled her eyes.

"Clara," said Marissa as she awkwardly flopped onto the coal pile, "you know you pretty much just saved my life back there, right?"

Clara shrugged. "Does that mean I can have your lava lamp?"

"Look sharp back there!" yelled a gruff voice.

"Sorry, Mr. Engineer," said Quentin, climbing down from the coal pile into the cab of the train's engine. Clara and Marissa followed. The train's engineer was a craggy-faced man, chewing on a sandwich. He didn't seem at all surprised to see Quentin and Clara.

"Pull that calf's tail, will ya?" said the man. "It's shining time!"

"Yes, sir!" cried Quentin happily. He jumped to his feet and yanked a chain, releasing a shrill blast of steam through the brass whistle.

"It was my turn to blow the whistle!" complained Clara.

"Bleed the pressure knob!" the engineer snapped.

"Okaaay," said Clara. She turned a copper wheel on the dashboard, and blasts of white steam shot out from both sides of the locomotive.

"Always fighting over a silly whistle while the boiler's like to explode," the engineer muttered to himself. "I've half a mind to turn this whole train around and take you both home."

"Sorry," both Clara and Quentin said.

"You there," said the engineer, pointing at Marissa, "release the brake."

Marissa looked at the large black lever to her right. The engineer nodded. She pulled it back, and the entire train shot forward.

"Hey, I never got to do that!" protested Quentin.

"CALF'S TAIL!" shouted the engineer. Quentin pulled the chain and another shrill scream shot out of the brass pipe.

"Bail it in!" yelled the engineer as he opened the metal door, revealing burning red coals in the firebox. Clara and Quentin grabbed shovels and took turns dumping coal into the fire. Marissa picked up a shovel and clumsily joined in. The engineer watched them all while attacking his sandwich.

Marissa leaned toward the other two and quietly asked, "How come he's not throwing us off?"

"We made friends with him," Clara replied cheerfully, hoisting another half shovelful of coal into the firebox.

Quentin nodded toward the engineer with a smile. Marissa looked again and saw that the sandwich he was eating was overflowing with ham and cheese. She saw Quentin's bundle lying open on a ledge.

"*Told* you it was good food!" said Quentin.

The engineer lifted the sandwich toward them in a mock

toast, then reached for the bundle and ripped off another corner of White House cheese.

The train rolled through the small towns and big cities of Ohio and Indiana, each time pausing at the station just long enough for the president to talk about crops of children, crops of corn, steel, industry, and progress. By the time they rolled out of South Bend, the sky was dark and the tracks were only visible in the circle of light shining out from the train's headlamp.

The moon glimmered on a large body of water to their right. The engineer pointed and shouted "Lake Michigan!" As they rounded the shore, an orange glow appeared to the north. The engineer shouted "Chicago!"

As they approached the city from the south, the air grew thick with smoke and sulfur, and they saw flames shooting from the tops of smokestacks. Flashes of red and orange shimmered from factories and steel mills, lighting up the tracks for mile after mile.

The train passed stockyards packed with cows and pigs. Giant grain elevators loomed over the tracks. Marissa's eyes watered at the thick animal smell hanging in the air, and her lungs stung with the haze of smoke and soot.

As they rolled alongside paved streets and brick houses, they saw more motorcars than they'd seen in Washington, and fewer horses. Long strings of small white lightbulbs formed words advertising theaters and restaurants, with the music of countless pianos, horns, and clarinets meeting in the air.

The ornate buildings were getting fancier now, each one of them with its own style, its own carvings and patterns and lighting, as if competing for the attention of the train rolling past. The buildings grew taller and tighter like the walls of a narrow canyon.

Then everything opened up. The train rumbled into a vast railyard, alongside dozens of other moving trains on parallel tracks. It seemed like the whole country was crashing together in this noisy and bustling place. Marissa looked out at the massive railyard and the glowing city rising beyond it. She thought about what Wendell had said: That, my friends, is your new century.

The engineer took control of the levers and wheels in the cab, carefully slowing the train's progress and guiding it into one of the black tunnels beneath an imposing stone building.

There were no bands playing when the train pulled into a dimly lit cavern of endless platforms and sleeping locomotives. No crowds to greet the president. Aside from scattered railroad employees and porters, the only people on the platform were three men in top hats and tuxedos, and six police officers in gold-buttoned blue woolen jackets.

Marissa instinctively ducked so she couldn't be seen from the platform. The engineer gave a hard laugh and said, "They're not here for you, miss. It's the big fellah they want."

As the engineer banked the ashes in the firebox and released the remaining steam from the locomotive, President Roosevelt came striding up the platform, also wearing a tuxedo and a top hat. Flanking him were Mr. Loeb, frowning as usual, and Wendell, smiling broadly.

The president trotted forward at the sight of the men waiting on the platform.

"MAAAAAYOR HARRISON!" he shouted, his high-pitched voice echoing off the high ceiling of the platform. "DEEE-LIGHTED!"

The youngest of the men on the platform stepped forward, removing his hat and bowing to the president as he approached. Roosevelt and Harrison hugged each other and walked arm in arm down the platform, chatting as if they were best friends since kindergarten, smiling broadly beneath matching mustaches.

"They really seem to like each other," said Clara.

"That man," grumbled Quentin, "plans to run against Father for president."

The police officers formed a wide walking bubble around the president and the mayor. The other men in tuxedos greeted Mr. Loeb and Wendell politely and followed at a respectful distance behind the two leaders.

The other train passengers fell in behind: senators, congress-men, businessmen, and reporters all mingled, distinguished only by the quality of their clothes. As this parade walked past the locomotive, Marissa caught sight of Alex Lee looking straight up at them. Marissa ducked out of sight.

"Nice knowin' ya," grunted the engineer as he gathered up a

small black bag and took the last hunk of cheese from Quentin's bandanna.

"You're leaving?" asked Quentin nervously.

"End of the line for me," said the engineer as he climbed down onto the platform. "You're on the spot for three hours, then a new crew will arrive for the push west." As he walked away, he said, "Mind you, they'll expect a clean coffeepot."

"Coffeepot?" Clara asked.

"That's railroad talk for the locomotive," Quentin said.

"Oh," said Marissa. "So we have to get out of here."

"Let's eat!" said Clara. "Think we can find some Chicago pizza?"

"What's pizza?" asked Quentin.

"You guys kill me," Clara muttered.

"We can't leave the train," said Marissa, eyeing the distant platform exit, where a tall police officer stood with his back turned to the train. "But I know where we can get some food. Come on." She picked up a flickering lantern and entered the baggage car.

"Where's Ethel?" asked Quentin.

Marissa looked around for a moment, then said, "I think I know." She led them into the press car. The corridor was empty and dark. The only sound in the car was the clinking of coins behind the second compartment door. Marissa slid open the door and found Ethel seated behind the poker table, counting her money.

"Oh hello," Ethel said calmly. She took a silver dollar from the top of one of her stacks and flipped it to Quentin, who caught it with a look of awe and quickly pocketed it.

"Come on," said Marissa, "let's get some food."

Ethel looked at the filthy clothes and windblown hair on Marissa, Quentin, and Clara. "Are you really going like that," asked Ethel, "for dinner with the president's daughter?"

CHAPTER 10

THE CABOOSE

THE four made their way to the dark and deserted dining car. The buffet table was empty, but in the small galley they found roast beef, cheese, vegetables, and dessert. They each piled plates high with food and settled in at a booth with a white tablecloth and fresh cut flowers.

After helping herself to a second slice of chocolate cake, Ethel casually announced that she knew Wendell's plans.

"So do I," said Marissa, unimpressed. "He's chopping the Steeple Giant down and building a dam."

Ethel looked at Marissa and asked, "Do you know what he's planning to do after that?"

"No."

"Hmm," said Ethel, taking a bite of her cake and looking out the window onto the dark and empty Chicago platform. "I do."

"How?" asked Clara.

Ethel turned and said, "I . . . what was the word you used, Quentin? I reconnoitered." She took another bite, then touched the corners of her lips with a white linen napkin.

"You spied?" Quentin said, mouth full of banana cream pie.

"I listened," said Ethel. "Mr. Wendell talks a lot when he plays cards. He said he will be the king of California after he's done carving up the mountains."

"Meaning what?" Marissa asked.

"More dams," said Ethel. "Dozens of them. Enough to power the whole coast. He said when Father's canal connects the Atlantic with the Pacific in Panama, California's cities will boom. They'll need more power. And more mines too. More factories." She scraped a bit of icing from her plate with the side of her fork. "He called it the next California Gold Rush. And he said Loeb will help him do it, because Father needs the votes out west."

Marissa remembered the conversation she'd overheard when she was hiding under the buffet in the dining car. Electricity! Wendell had said. Industry! Dam the Sierras!

"Wonder how many more giant sequoias he'll cut to make that happen," muttered Marissa.

"All of them," said Ethel as she got up to refill her plate.

"*What*?" said Clara.

"Wendell has secured the timber rights for the whole northern Sierra mountain range," said Ethel. "And he plans on harvesting it all to make room for progress."

"Not all of them," said Marissa. "I mean, we know he won't knock down all the big trees."

"How do we know that?" asked Ethel with an arched eyebrow.

"Because we, I mean, they're still there! In the future I mean. We took all these hikes, me and Clara, and there were big trees,

and . . ." Her voice trailed off as she saw the look exchanged between Ethel and Quentin.

Ethel smiled sympathetically. "It doesn't—"

"Ethel," said Marissa through gritted teeth, "if you say 'It doesn't work that way' to me again, I'm throwing you off this train."

"Be that as it may," said Ethel, securing a slice of apple pie and returning to the table, "it doesn't work that way."

"Throw her off!" Quentin exclaimed with a gap-toothed smile. "Throw her off!"

Clara picked up the chant. "Throw her off! Throw her off!"

"Just because you remember something from your time," said Ethel, ignoring them, "doesn't mean it will necessarily be so—that is to say, without your help. You can't just count on things working out without your involvement, any more than you could in your own time."

"So," said Marissa, the chocolate strawberry in her mouth suddenly tasting like dust, "if we screw this up, there won't be *any* of the big trees when we get back home?"

"Indeed," said Ethel. She took a bite of her apple pie and smiled. "I must say it's a pleasure eating a good meal without Mother and Alice constantly looking over my shoulder."

"One tree," said Marissa. "That was the mission. Don't put every redwood on my shoulders."

Ethel shrugged and enjoyed another bite of apple pie. "Who knows, maybe your mission is more than the big trees," she said cheerily. "Wendell also said he's secured mining rights to the Grand Canyon."

"Stop it, OK?" said Marissa, throwing her napkin on the table and standing up. "Just . . . where'd you say he's got these plans?"

"Locked in Mr. Loeb's office, I'd imagine," replied Ethel calmly.

"That's in the caboose," said Quentin, confidently showing off more of his train knowledge.

Marissa stormed off down the length of the dining car, with Clara running after her. They passed through the first-class passenger car, then crossed over to the president's car, finding it locked. Marissa climbed down onto the platform to walk around, but Clara climbed up the narrow metal ladder to the roof. She ran to the other end, leaping fearlessly over the gap and onto the caboose roof.

Marissa walked down the silent platform and felt a slight chill upon seeing the back of the caboose again. She reached up for the railing, hoisted herself over, and tried the caboose door.

Locked.

Marissa sighed and turned to face the empty tracks extending into the pitch-black tunnel behind the train. She was standing exactly where President Roosevelt had spoken at stop after stop along the way. Marissa pictured the adoring faces looking up expectantly, pressing against the back of the train, cheering and laughing and applauding.

There was a loud thud inside the caboose. Marissa spun around. The caboose door slid open and Clara stuck her head out.

Marissa stared at her sister, confused.

"I climbed down through the cupola!" Clara said.

"What?"

Clara pointed up at the windowed opening in the roof of the caboose. "That's called a cupola!"

"You've been spending too much time with Quentin," said Marissa, and she entered the small office inside the caboose.

In the shadows was a wooden desk covered with papers, and a framed black-and-white photograph showing a serious-looking Mr. Loeb and his equally serious-looking family.

The caboose door slid shut behind her.

Clara climbed on top of the desk and hoisted herself back onto the roof through the cupola.

Marissa lit a candle. There were several wooden file cabinets and a small wooden table surrounded by chairs, with a half-smoked cigar stubbed out in the ashtray, still giving off a faint trail of smoke.

On the wall was a large map of the United States, with the train's route sketched out in a long, snaking line of black ink. The portions that had already been completed, from Washington to Chicago, were checked off with neat marks. Beyond Chicago the route went much farther, heading through Wisconsin, Minnesota, North Dakota, and Wyoming, eventually looping down into California through the Sierras before reaching the ocean at San Francisco.

On the table, next to the ashtray, was a short stack of folders with handwritten labels on the tabs. Near the bottom of a stack, one folder caught Marissa's eye. It was labeled *Wendell Power Dam.*

Marissa pulled the folder out and opened it to several documents and a small map printed on letterhead from the Arnold Wendell Engineering Company, San Francisco, California.

Above her, Marissa could hear Clara's feet thumping along the top of the car.

Marissa unfolded the map. There were marks and notes in tight cursive letters, with numbers and dates alongside pictures of a dam, a creek, and the wavy outlines of a planned lake engulfing nearly everything shown. Next to the creek was a cabin marked *abandoned,* and across from it was a single tree marked *Steeple Giant (Remove)*.

"Marissa!" hissed Clara's voice from above. "Somebody's coming! Get out of there!"

Clara closed the cupola window and thumped away. Marissa opened the door at the back of the caboose, but quickly shut it again upon seeing several workmen nearby. She was trapped in the caboose, at least for now. She looked back at the table.

There was another folder, marked *Wendell Sierra Power Network*. Inside the folder was another map, this one showing the whole state of California. Running along the eastern side of the state were dozens of circles, each indicating a planned power dam, turning the Sierras into a long chain of man-made lakes. Ethel was right. The dam that would eliminate the Steeple Giant would be just the first of many.

There were voices outside on the platform.

Marissa moved over to the door and slid the lock shut. She propped a chair against the door handle.

The heavy boots of workmen stomped past along the platform.

Marissa returned to the table and looked closer at the scribblings next to the lakes. She found a magnifying glass on Mr. Loeb's desk and held it over the writing. There were planned towns and cities, farms and ranches, factories and mines surrounding every dam. The entire mountain range was covered with these plans.

A pair of dress shoes clicked along the platform and stepped behind the door.

Marissa lifted the candle to blow out the flame. But then her eye caught a Western Union telegram sticking out of one of the folders.

TO W LOEB FROM A WENDELL, read the first line, pasted to a yellow card.

REQUIRE PRESIDENTS ASSISTANCE TO CLEAR RESISTANCE TO DEVELOPMENT, said the next.

The back door rattled.

NATIONS FUTURE DEPENDS ON OPENING SIERRAS FOR POWER AND ECONOMY

Keys jangled outside the door.

PRESIDENTS FUTURE DEPENDS ON SECURING CALIFORNIA DELEGATES

The lock clicked open. The handle turned, but jammed against the chair. Air whistled in through the crack in the door and the flame of the candle flickered. Marissa's eyes caught the final lines of the telegram.

CUT WHAT WE CAN

BURN WHAT WE CANT

BLAST WHATS LEFT

Another burst of air swept in from the crack in the door, blowing out the candle and plunging the tiny office into darkness. The door rattled hard against the obstructing chair.

"What the devil is this?" muttered Mr. Loeb's voice through the door at the back of the car. In the darkness of the office, Marissa shoved the telegram and the maps back into the folder and tucked it under her arm, then slipped out the other door in the front, into the space between the caboose and the president's car.

There were many voices in the air now, as railroad workers hurried back and forth preparing the train for departure. There was no way to sneak out onto the crowded platform unnoticed. Marissa looked up at the top of the president's car and briefly considered pulling a Clara. But the roof was out of the question with this many people around.

Marissa reached for the president's car and pulled the handle.

CHAPTER 11

THE ARENA

THE door to President Roosevelt's personal railroad car slid open. Flickering lanterns lined the shiny mahogany walls, casting a shadowy warmth over the white lace curtains and the brass fixtures. The shades were drawn over the large picture windows, but Marissa could hear the activity outside as the platform bustled with rolling wagons and hurrying footsteps. A loud blast of steam sounded farther up the train as the locomotive prepared for departure.

Marissa moved down the narrow corridor, passing ornate bathrooms and comfortable bedrooms. One bedroom door was closed. The corridor opened into a wood-paneled dining room. In the center was a formal table, piled high with books and papers and an old cavalry hat, plus a stuffed falcon mounted on a wooden stick. Hanging by one of the windows was a battered leather boxing bag. In the corner, by the exit, was a small closet, its door hanging open to reveal several fishing poles and a folded canvas tent.

The whistle blew once, then blew again right away, then a third time right after that, and the train started to move, sending Marissa tumbling to the plush carpet floor. She looked around, surprised that the train was already moving when it seemed like preparations had only just begun.

Marissa remembered the hurry-up-and-wait atmosphere on Air Force One whenever she traveled with her mom. Sometimes the plane engines would spin for hours, turning fuel into noise, waiting for the president to show up. Other times it was a mad scramble from silence to the runway in two minutes.

That's because whenever the president got on board, whether early or late, the doors closed and the wheels rolled. If you weren't inside when that happened, tough luck. It must be the same thing on this train, Marissa thought. Teddy was on board.

And if Teddy was on board, Teddy was probably in his car.

Marissa remembered the closed door she'd walked past.

And now that door was sliding open.

Marissa ran toward the end of the car, but the train swayed and knocked her off balance, sending her hurtling into the small closet, where she fell into the canvas of the folded tent. The fishing rods tumbled on top of her.

Now hidden beneath a jumble of camping and fishing equipment, Marissa held still, watching the hallway. There was a sharp crack. Followed by another, and another, and another.

President Roosevelt bounced into view, jumping rope up the narrow hall, oblivious to Marissa's presence. He tossed the rope aside and took a hard swing at the battered leather boxing bag, followed by another, and another. After ten minutes, he stepped away and dropped to the floor, neatly executing fifty push-ups, then fifty sit-ups. He dropped into a chair at the table and went through a tall stack of papers, grumbling and grunting and signing, over and over again. He read a book, flipping through the pages every ten seconds. He read another. Marissa's eyes grew heavy as the train continued rocking into the night.

Finally Roosevelt stood, yawned, did another fifty push-ups, then stomped off down the hall. Marissa waited to hear his door close so she could slip out to the exit. But the president wasn't ready for sleep. Roosevelt returned to the table, carefully carrying a closed wooden box. There was a spring in his step that hadn't been there before, an excitement in his movements as he opened the box, eyes wide, a childish smile beneath his mustache.

He gently lifted the stuffed falcon from the table and studied it from every angle. He picked up a charcoal pencil from the box and started patiently sketching the bird in front of him. Marissa remembered the book Alex Lee had been reading, with its beautiful illustrations of birds and wildlife. By Theodore Roosevelt.

Roosevelt worked with intense concentration, but he looked happier, more relaxed, than he had all day. He took out a set of watercolors and carefully brushed colors into the sketch he'd completed. Marissa settled in against the tent in the closet, watching Roosevelt paint, until sleep overtook her.

When Marissa awoke, Roosevelt was gone. Early morning light filtered in behind the shades of the window. Marissa slowly untangled herself from under the pile of tent cloth and fishing rods, trying not to make a sound. She tiptoed to the exit door and slipped out into the cold morning air. Blinking the sleep out of her eyes, she stepped over the open gap to the first-class car.

"Smell that?" President Roosevelt yelled behind her over the howling wind and the clattering wheels.

Marissa spun around.

Roosevelt was dressed in a rugged western outfit. The old cavalry hat was perched on his head. He was lounging on the metal bench outside the door to his car, his old, worn boots resting on the railing, his eyes fixed on the cold gray scenery passing by.

"The western wind!" Roosevelt shouted. He took a deep breath.

Marissa pressed her back against the first-class door and held on tightly to its handle. She wasn't sure if Roosevelt thought she'd just come from the first-class car or if he knew she'd been trespassing in his own car. His eyes were fixed on the passing horizon.

"You do smell it, don't you?" asked Roosevelt. "The pine trees of the Rockies? The cattle of Dakota? The frozen lakes of Minnesota? The western wind carries it all!"

Marissa breathed in. All she smelled was cold.

Roosevelt took another deep breath and closed his eyes with a smile. "The Great North Woods of Wisconsin!" Then he opened his eyes, and the smile faded as he looked out over the passing hills, covered with nothing but dead stumps. "Well, they used to be great, anyhow."

The train rattled along. Roosevelt tugged thoughtfully at the end of his mustache, looking a little lost and sad.

When he finally spoke, he said, "The first time I passed through here, you couldn't see more than ten feet ahead, the trees were so thick." He shook his head. "I was a lot younger then. So was the country."

Marissa looked out at the barren hills as the first rays of sunlight emerged from behind the train. "Why . . . ?" she asked.

"The country must be allowed to grow," said Roosevelt.

"Yeah, but . . ." said Marissa, her voice fading away.

They rode in silence for a few minutes. The hills gave way to a valley, also covered in dead stumps. Running through the valley was a river, filled with logs. As the hill rose on the other side, the land took on a scorched appearance, with hundreds more tree stumps that had been burned to clear land. The land began to slope downward, and a stream appeared alongside the train.

Roosevelt gestured at the brown water. "Same thing I had to fight when I was governor of New York," he said. "Mind you, there's nothing I enjoy more than lumbering. I've got nine axes of my own back on Long Island. But when there's no trees at all, there's nothing to prevent the topsoil from washing away."

He dropped his feet from the railing and stood up for a better view. He held on and leaned out, peering into the distance beyond the train. "So all the good farmland ends up . . . there," he said, "floating away down the Mississippi."

The train curved and a mighty river swung into view, glittering in the early morning sunlight. A white riverboat, three stories high, was churning upriver with a wide red paddlewheel, puffs of black smoke rising in a steady pattern from the chimneys.

A bird soared above the boat. Roosevelt watched it enthusiastically. "Double-crested cormorant," he said confidently. "Watching the boat's wake to see if it turns up breakfast."

Roosevelt and Marissa watched in silence as the bird soared on the rising air, eyes set on the water, waiting to pounce. Suddenly the bird plunged from the sky, wings tucked, straight down into the water with stunning speed. And up it came with a helpless fish flopping from its beak.

"BULLY!" Roosevelt shouted with delight, as if he were the one who'd just scored the perfect kill. He watched the bird admiringly as it flew off. "Makes its nest high in the treetops."

"But there are no treetops," Marissa said, looking at the barren shoreline.

Roosevelt waved her off. "Birds are resilient. Adaptable." He frowned, looking a little off balance. "Even migratory patterns can . . ." he said softly as his voice trailed away.

He shook his head sadly and looked back at the stumps and scorches punctuating the Wisconsin riverside. He shook his fist in agitation. "Confound it, child, there's only so much a president can do!"

Marissa, surprised by this outburst, said nothing.

Roosevelt glowered back at the rolling hillsides.

"Progress must advance," he said, sounding like he was attempting to convince himself more than her. "With the crowned heads of Europe all building industries and ships, American cannot be left . . ."

Then he looked at Marissa, and his eyebrows lowered. "I know you."

Marissa tried to keep her expression blank.

"You were mixed up in that little horse caper back at the White House, were you not?" asked Roosevelt.

Noticing the panicked look that crossed Marissa's face, he added, "I assume your presence on this train is not authorized?"

Marissa shook her head.

"And that it took some act of great daring?"

Marissa shrugged.

"Good on you!" he said with a grin. "This train is packed with too many spectators, not enough spirits of action!" He stuck his chin out contemptuously at the first-class car in front of them. "Cold and timid souls they are," he said, "who neither know victory nor defeat."

The train slowed as it approached the bridge crossing the Mississippi River. Roosevelt stood and stretched without holding on to anything.

"It's not the critic who counts," he said. "Do you understand?"

"I guess," said Marissa. She had no idea what he was talking about.

Roosevelt nodded thoughtfully as the train rumbled onto the trestle and began to cross the wide river.

"The credit," he said, as much to himself as Marissa, "belongs to the man in the arena."

"What arena?" Marissa asked.

"Why, the arena of life!" said Roosevelt. "The credit goes to the ones with faces covered in dust and sweat and blood. The ones who know the triumph of achievement!"

He looked back at the clear-cut hills of Wisconsin and let out a heavy sigh, before adding, "Or if they fail, at least fail while daring greatly." He fixed a hard stare at Marissa, teeth bared, mustache bristling, and raised a finger, like a military officer giving a command. "Dare," he said.

He turned and walked into his personal car. As he disappeared behind the closing door, he shouted, "Dare greatly!" The door clicked shut and Roosevelt was gone.

Marissa watched the reflection of the train on the river below. The train reached the other side of the bridge and curved up along the west riverbank. The whistle blew and a small Minnesota river town rolled into view. A band played. Flags waved. People cheered.

When the train came to a complete stop, Marissa climbed out onto the crowded platform and found the pack of sleepy reporters making their way through the crowd for the first speech of the day. Alex Lee saw Marissa and grabbed her arm, pulling her into the center of the pack.

On the back deck of the caboose, Roosevelt was already talking, energetic as ever, waving, and grinning in the bright sunshine. He gave his usual speech, thanking veterans of the Civil War, greeting his fellow veterans of the Spanish-American War, congratulating the farmers on their crops and families on their crops of children. He talked about progress, development, industry. All of the things he'd said before.

But as the locomotive began building steam, Roosevelt added, "However, as we speak of progress, I must add a word of caution."

Up ahead, Marissa saw Mr. Loeb look up.

"I had occasion to speak this morning with a girl," said Roosevelt.

Marissa smiled. Alex Lee noticed and raised an eyebrow.

"She saw the remains of a dead forest," said Roosevelt, "and asked a simple question: 'Why?' That simple question reminded me of a simple truth."

The reporters opened their notebooks. This was new.

Roosevelt put his finger in the air and said, "Our nation has become great because of the lavish use of our resources. But the time has come to inquire seriously what will happen when our forests are gone, when the coal, the iron, the oil, and the gas are exhausted, when the soils have still further impoverished and washed into the streams, polluting the rivers, denuding the fields, and obstructing navigation."

Marissa saw Wendell walk over to Mr. Loeb. He said something while waving his hands in agitation. Mr. Loeb ignored him, and cast a suspicious gaze down the platform.

CHAPTER 12

A MOONLIGHT STROLL

THE whistle blew and the reporters scrambled back onto the press car, with Marissa right in the middle.

"Ever played poker, kid?" asked Phillips as the train jerked forward.

"No," said Marissa.

"Great, maybe we can win back some of the bread we lost to the other two."

"Other two?" asked Marissa as they arrived at the compartment.

Ethel sat amid the reporters with a pile of money in front of her. And in the next seat over, behind a smaller pile, was Clara.

"*There* you are, darling," said Ethel when she saw Marissa. "Have you met my sister?"

"Your sister?" asked Marissa.

She heard voices in the corridor. She looked out the door and saw Mr. Loeb talking to two men in suits and bowler hats. Marissa ducked back into the poker compartment and hissed, "He's coming!"

Marissa jumped into the empty bunk above the crowded table.

Clara jumped up from her seat and followed Marissa onto the bunk, with Ethel right behind her. The three huddled under a rough wool blanket.

"You play poker now?" Marissa whispered to her sister.

"Ethel's a good teacher," Clara whispered.

"Clara is annoyingly lucky," added Ethel, "but sneaky enough to check-raise pocket cowboys."

"What?" whispered Marissa.

"You wouldn't understand," Clara whispered back.

Mr. Loeb's voice entered the compartment. "How is the press this morning?"

"Tired!" yelled Burns.

Mr. Loeb gave a dry laugh. "Only twelve more stops today."

"Hey, Loeb," said Gordon, "what gives with that song and dance he gave at the end of the speech about the forest?"

"Is he going to make it illegal to chop wood?" asked Burns.

"Of course not," said Mr. Loeb. "The president believes the future of this country depends on harvesting our resources without restriction."

"Yeah," said Burns, "but he said he talked to a girl this morning. Which girl?"

"Obviously a figure of speech," said Mr. Loeb. "This was the first stop of the day—he couldn't possibly have . . ." Mr. Loeb's voice trailed off.

Under the blanket, Clara could hear him stepping closer. "I'm sorry," his voice said, closer now, "did you say 'Which girl?'"

"Why, sure," said Burns, "there's kids all over this train—OW!"

"Sorry," said Gordon. "My foot slipped. Into your shin."

"What kids?" Mr. Loeb asked coldly.

"Some rug rats tried to get on board in Chicago," said Phillips. "We chased them off for you."

"Interesting," said Mr. Loeb, his voice closer to the bunk. "I'll thank you to alert me from now on if you encounter any more . . . young passengers."

"Sure," said Gordon. "We'll get right on that."

"And," continued Mr. Loeb, leaning against the upper bunk now, just inches away from the blanket covering the girls, "I expect your complete cooperation with our new security team."

"New?" asked Burns.

"Mr. Pinkerton was unavoidably detained in Youngstown," said Mr. Loeb.

"Because he went berserk and jumped into the crowd during the president's speech?" asked Gordon.

"Be that as it may," said Mr. Loeb, "there remains a need for professional security. I regret to inform you there is evidence on this train of recent unauthorized access."

"Sounds like a swell story . . ." said Gordon, pulling out his notebook.

"I have no further comment," replied Mr. Loeb. "But I'd like to introduce you to our new team, who I am confident will handle all concerns. Jeffrey?"

Clara heard a set of boots walk into the compartment, with another set of boots right behind it.

"Which one is Jeffrey?" asked Gordon.

"I am," two stern voices replied at the same time.

"You two related?" asked Burns.

"No," they both answered.

"This is Jeffrey John," said Mr. Loeb. "And that is Jonathan Jeffrey."

"Hey, Jeffrey!" said Gordon.

"Yes?" they both responded.

Gordon giggled in delight. "Play cards?"

"No," replied one.

"You must be the fun one," Phillips said.

"No," replied the other.

"Thanks for the introduction, Loeb," said Gordon. "I can tell these fellows will be a joy."

The back of Clara's throat started to itch. Mr. Loeb remained right next to the bunk.

"So, uh, happy hunting!" Gordon said.

Again, no one moved.

"Thanks for the visit," added Burns, a nervous twinge to his voice. "If you'll excuse us, we have important . . . cards to—"

"I wonder," said Mr. Loeb, his voice right above the lumpy blanket that hid Clara, Marissa, and Ethel, "where one might hide on this train, if one didn't want to be found."

"I don't know," said Gordon, "but if I keep losing money to these cardsharps, I'll have to find out!"

The reporters laughed loudly. Too loudly, thought Clara. Pressure built behind her nose.

"We'll be sure to tell you if we see anything," said Phillips.

The train lurched. And Clara sneezed.

Outside the wheels continued to rattle, and a clanging bell passed by.

"GESUNDHEIT!" yelled Gordon.

"Yeah," said Phillips. "Bless you, Clement. Nasty sneeze you got there."

"This is Mr. Clement?" Mr. Loeb's voice said over the blanket.

"Sure, that's right," said Gordon. "He's been really sick after he ate some bad clams in Chicago."

"Clams indeed," muttered Mr. Loeb. "Jeffrey, please remove the blanket."

"I'd . . . rather not," said a voice.

"Smart move," said Gordon. "He's kind of a mess."

"Never seen snot that green," said Phillips.

"More of an olive color, really," said Gordon.

"Rotting slug belly," said Phillips. "In the hot sun."

The whistle blew, and the train began to slow.

"All right, gentlemen," said Mr. Loeb. "As I must prepare for the next stop, I'll leave it be. For now. Please give . . . Mr. Clement . . . my wishes for a speedy recovery."

Three sets of footsteps left the compartment. Someone got up and slid the door shut. Bright sunlight flashed in Clara's eyes as the blanket was yanked off the three girls.

"OK, ladies," said Phillips, "we covered for you, but what gives?"

"You on the lam?" asked Gordon. "Hiding from the law?"

"Naw," said Burns, pulling at his suspenders. "I make them for lost princesses."

"Are you gonna tell on us?" asked Clara.

The reporters all laughed. "What, to that undertaker Loeb?" asked Gordon. "Listen, kid, thing you have to learn about reporters is, the only way to make us keep a secret, is to tell us we can't."

"And when a guy like Loeb says we have to turn you in," said Phillips, sitting back down at the card game, "well, that kinda makes you family now."

"Hey," said Gordon, pointing at Marissa, "that was you this morning, wasn't it?"

"Me?" Marissa asked.

"The one who got the president talking about saving the forests and such," said Gordon. "I remember you had a bee in your bonnet about that hill fire back in Pennsylvania. Finally got a chance to bug old Teddy about it, didn't you?"

"Um, maybe," said Marissa.

Gordon scratched his muttonchop beard thoughtfully. "I'm impressed," he said, "but don't be surprised if that's the last time you hear the president talk that way."

"What do you mean?" asked Clara.

"I'm just saying," said Gordon, "there's a lot of people on this train who don't like anyone telling them they can't cut a tree or dig a mine."

When the train stopped in Saint Paul, Gordon's prediction seemed to have come true. The president spoke about building more factories along the Mississippi. In Minneapolis he talked about iron, steel, and a new navy. In Sioux Falls, with Wendell smiling in approval, the president declared that nothing should stand in the way of generating the most electricity possible.

In every small town and big city along the way, Roosevelt talked about progress, development, and industry. There was no more talk about impoverished soil or polluted rivers.

As the cold baggage car rolled into the night, Quentin snored on a luggage rack, and Ethel slept inside a trunk with her thick bag of money. As Clara and Marissa snuggled on a pile of duffel bags, Marissa described her early morning conversation with Teddy Roosevelt.

"'Dare greatly,'" Clara said, repeating the line Roosevelt had said to Marissa. "I like that."

"He was pretty intense."

"But why does it have to be 'the *man* in the arena'?" asked Clara.

"I don't know," Marissa replied in a sleepy voice. "I was too busy trying to avoid becoming the kid on the train tracks."

"How come he stopped talking about the trees?" asked Clara.

"Politics, I guess," said Marissa, yawning. "They got to him, like Gordon said they would." She rolled over.

"What are we going to do?" asked Clara.

Marissa didn't answer. She was already asleep.

Between the noise of the train and Quentin's snoring, Clara was awake for hours. In the middle of the night, the train pulled to a stop. Clara heard water sloshing into the tank. She also heard footsteps crunching on the gravel outside.

A surprised voice toward the front of the train called out, "Hello, Mr. President."

"Fine hour for a walk, is it not?" the voice of President Roosevelt responded.

"Certainly, sir," said the other voice. "We're just about done taking on water, but if you'd like to walk more . . ."

"Yes, Mr. Engineer, sir," said Roosevelt, "I haven't walked a Dakota night for decades. Give me another moment, would you?"

"Of course, sir."

Clara quietly slipped out of the baggage car. In the silver moonlight she saw the president walk by in his western jacket and crushed cowboy hat, with thick leather work gloves on his hands. She watched as he strolled down the tracks, whistling and gazing at the stars.

Clara heard the latch click on the door behind her. She scrambled up the ladder to avoid being seen, and crawled to the top of the baggage car. A large metal pipe was suspended over the locomotive, noisily refilling its water tank.

Clara looked toward the back of the train and saw Alex Lee emerge from the press car, hat pulled low, peeking out between cars to watch Roosevelt on his midnight stroll.

As Clara spied on the reporter, the reporter spied on Roosevelt, who ran a gloved hand along the top of a barbed wire fence separating the tracks from the rolling plain. When he reached a break in the fence, Roosevelt expertly pulled the lengths of fence together and repaired the gap.

"I see you know how to wire, sir," the engineer called down from the locomotive.

"That I do," said Roosevelt. "I spent many a day stringing barbs across my Elkhorn ranch not thirty miles from here."

"I was a ranch hand myself once too, you know," replied the engineer.

"Consider yourself blessed," said Roosevelt. "To my mind, there's no better education than the hard life of the Dakota Badlands. It taught me self-reliance, hardihood, and the value of instant decision."

The wind howled over the dark landscape.

"About as lonely here now as when you were ranching, eh, Mr. President?" asked the engineer.

"More fences now," grumbled Roosevelt, "but the western wind still speaks."

"Yes, sir," said the engineer. "That it does."

"Thank goodness for that," said the president. "Good night."

"Good night, Mr. President," said the engineer.

Clara stood on top of the baggage car, shrouded in the smoke drifting back from the locomotive. The water from the big pipe continued gushing. Clara watched Roosevelt walk by below as Alex Lee watched from the shadows. Then the reporter went inside and Roosevelt continued down the tracks.

Clara took a few steps back, then ran toward the end of the baggage car and leapt over the gap to the press car. She landed with a thud, but the sound was covered by a blast of steam from the locomotive. She crawled along the top of the car until she was right next to where Roosevelt was mending another break in the fence.

As his hands expertly joined the loose pieces of sharp wire into barbed points, Roosevelt whistled to himself. He moved on to another break in the fence, farther down the line, and Clara ran after him, leaping to the top of the dining car. This time he heard the thud as she landed, and looked up.

"Someone there?" Roosevelt asked.

Clara held still.

"Show yourself, bandit!" said Roosevelt.

The wind swept across the tall grass. Roosevelt held his hat and looked into the swirling darkness.

"Ah," said Roosevelt, facing the wind, "just you, old friend."

He turned his attention back to the fence, finished his work, and waved his hat to the engineer up ahead.

The whistle sounded in response, and smoke began puffing from the locomotive. The train jerked forward. Roosevelt took several quick steps and casually swung himself aboard the moving train.

Above him, Clara dropped into a crouch to keep her balance. The curved metal roof under her feet rocked back and forth as the train picked up speed. The thickening smoke slid back along the top of the train, enveloping Clara in a gray haze. Orange sparks danced back through the smoke like flying dragons. Clara grinned as she surfed the train with ease.

Then a horizontal shadow burst into view through the smoke. The big water pipe was still hanging over the train. Clara tried to duck, but the large pipe caught her in the ribs. It knocked her off her feet and sent her tumbling back toward the end of the car. Her fingers scraped the metal roof as she tried to stop rolling, but it was no use.

Her momentum carried her right over the edge.

She landed, soft and secure. She opened her eyes. She was still on the train. In the space between the cars. In the arms of President Roosevelt, who was staring at her in wide-eyed shock.

"Another one," Roosevelt breathed in astonishment.

Clara's side throbbed in pain, and her breath came out in gasps. "Hi!" she squeaked.

Roosevelt put Clara back on her feet, on the ledge of the car facing him. His mouth moved in stunned silence. "What were you doing up there?" he managed to squeak.

Still gasping for air, Clara wondered what to say. Spying? "Daring," she coughed.

"DARING?" Roosevelt demanded over the noise of the train. The Black Hills rolled by behind him in the distant moonlight.

"Yeah," Clara said, her voice coming back to her. "You said . . . dare . . . greatly."

Roosevelt frowned. "I did, did I?"

"Yeah," Clara said.

She straightened up, trying to ignore the sharp ache in her side. She pointed at Roosevelt. "You should dare more, too." She coughed painfully. "I dare you."

"Now, who do you—"

"Stand up to that Wendell jerk," said Clara. "I double dare you."

She opened the door and started painfully skipping away toward the baggage car.

"Who *are* you?" asked Roosevelt.

She turned and giggled through the pain. "I'm the girl in the arena!"

CHAPTER 13

FERDINAND

"MOO."

"Shush."

"Mooooooooooooooooooooooo."

"Quentin, I'm trying to sleep!"

"That wasn't me!"

"Moooooo. Moo. Mooooooooo."

Marissa opened her eyes and looked around. Daylight streamed in through the cracks of the baggage car's wooden siding. The train was crawling. A chorus of mooing sounds and stomping feet and clanking bells surrounded the baggage car. Marissa hurried over to one of the cracks and looked out.

"COWS!" she exclaimed.

"You've never seen a cow before?" asked Ethel.

"Cows!" repeated Marissa. "I mean, really, cows! And . . . COWS!"

Ethel rolled her eyes and stepped over Clara's sleeping body to join Marissa. Ethel looked through the crack and said, "Oh my."

"What?" asked Quentin.

"Cows," Ethel said.

Marissa opened the door and went out into the space between the baggage car and the press car. She saw cows.

Thousands of cows.

A wide, hazy dome of dust and seeds rose around the herd, filling the air as completely as the constant noise of mooing, clanking, and stomping.

The train's whistle blew, again and again, as the train crept slowly forward through the herd. Marissa could hear the engineer up ahead, screaming himself hoarse to clear the tracks. The cows kept walking.

Each of the cows had magnificent horns, extending maybe three feet in either direction. They were unlike any cows Marissa had ever seen. Each cow had a different pattern of white splashed on brown, huge folds of skin extending almost to the ground, massive snouts reaching down to nip at the thin grass by the track bed.

"Longhorns!" gasped Quentin as he joined Marissa outside the baggage car. "Real Texas longhorns!"

"We're in *Texas*?" Marissa asked.

"No, ma'am," said a man in a cowboy hat as he rode by on a black horse, urging the slow-moving cattle along. "Medora!" He tipped his hat and rode past the train.

Quentin's face split into a gap-toothed grin. "Medora!" he gasped. "Ethel!" he yelled into the baggage car. "Medora!"

Ethel stuck her head out with an awestruck smile as the herd of cows passed by and a western town rolled into view. A large band played. A huge crowd roared. A gigantic banner hung over the platform reading: WELCOME HOME TEDDY!

"Medora!" shouted Ethel.

"What's Medora?" asked Marissa.

"Father lived here when he was a cowboy!" Ethel squeaked.

"Archie and Kermit and Ted will be so jealous!" yelled Quentin.

"Alice will just *die*!" added Ethel with a wicked grin.

Before the train had even come to a full stop in the small town of Medora, North Dakota, Quentin and Ethel jumped out onto the crowded platform and ran up the dusty dirt street beyond. Marissa jumped off after them, but lost them as the pack of reporters engulfed her, sweeping her toward the back of the train, where President Roosevelt was already speaking.

"I'm DEEEEEEEEEEEEEEEEEEE-lighted to be back!" He reached out and shook every hand and cried, "My HAPPIEST days were spent living here with you all!"

The crowd cheered. Marissa saw Alex Lee look up sharply.

An old cowboy shouted, "Saddle up, greenhorn!"

No one laughed harder at the insult than the president himself, who said, "Oh would that I could. It's been so long!"

He looked at the faces with wide, gleaming eyes and said, "A whole generation has been born and grown up since I rode guard around the cattle by your side. Little boys and girls now have children of their own!"

His face became more serious and his eyes narrowed. "And last night I had a . . . daring . . . inspiration, about these children, and the generations to come."

Alex Lee broke away from the crowd and Marissa followed, watching as the reporter wandered out into the deserted town, staring at the one- and two-story wooden buildings with the same look of wonder and excitement that had covered Quentin and Ethel's faces. The reporter reached down and scooped up a handful of dirt, sifting it carefully through gloved fingers like it was gold dust.

"My friends and neighbors," shouted President Roosevelt, "I recognize the right and duty of this generation to develop and use the natural resources of our land." He brought his fist down forcefully on the railing of the caboose. "But I do not recognize the right to waste them, or rob, by wasteful use, the generations that come after us."

Marissa looked up in surprise. Somehow the president was back to talking about conservation. The people clapped politely. Behind Roosevelt, Wendell threw his hands up in obvious frustration. Mr. Loeb stepped toward the railing and scanned the crowd suspiciously.

Marissa ducked behind a passing cow. She watched as Mr. Loeb summoned the Jeffreys, gesturing angrily. One of the men walked through the crowd, while the other began searching the train, heading toward the baggage car.

Marissa sprinted between cows, horses, and people to reach the baggage car first. She scrambled inside and shook Clara awake. "We gotta go."

Clara squinted hard. "Leave me alone," she groaned, holding her bruised side.

"Come on!" said Marissa. "Get up!"

"Nah."

"Code red!" said Marissa. "Sugar is *red*!"

Clara opened a skeptical eye and scowled. She grudgingly followed Marissa to the door.

They emerged into the sunlight. And ran right into one of the Jeffreys.

"STOP!" the Jeffrey yelled as the girls jumped out onto the platform and ran into the crowd of ranchers and families. They reached a tall wooden fence at the end of the street, which Clara smoothly vaulted over. Marissa struggled to lift herself over the dry, brittle wood but finally made it over.

The other side was a farther drop, to a sunken meadow several feet lower than the street. The entire meadow was surrounded by the tall wooden fence. Rising above the fence at the far side of the field was the black smokestack of the locomotive.

"Come on," said Marissa. "We'll sneak back on the coffeepot."

Clara shook her head, staring fearfully at something else. Marissa looked across the grass. It was another longhorn, all by itself. It had shorter horns than the others she'd seen. Hooked forward. And they framed a smoldering face that glared at the girls from across the field.

"I don't think that cow likes us," said Clara nervously.

"That's not a cow," said Marissa. "It's a bull."

Clara's fingers tightened on Marissa's arm. "Why did you have to say that?"

"Hello, Mr. Bull," Marissa said in a calm, sweet voice, "we're not here to bother you . . ."

The bull snorted, then lowered its head. And bit the grass.

"See?" Marissa said quietly. "He's just grazing. Like Ferdinand. You remember that story? Ferdinand just wanted to smell flowers," said Marissa.

The bull looked up and snorted with menacing eyes.

"That's not Ferdinand!" Clara cried.

The bull took several steps toward them, sniffing with agitation, looking above them.

"You there!" called a voice from the top of the fence behind them. "Stop this instant!"

Marissa looked up and saw the Jeffrey, pointing at her. He clumsily fell over the fence, landing seat-first onto the field. His bowler hat fell off, revealing bright red hair.

"Watch out!" Marissa warned him.

"You're not in a position to give orders, young lady," said the Jeffrey as he stood up and put his hat back on, oblivious to the massive bull approaching him.

"But sir—" said Marissa as the bull broke into a trot.

"Marissa!" cried Clara anxiously.

"You are guilty of trespassing! I saw you on the president's train!" said the Jeffrey, angrily straightening his tie. "Do you know what happens when you go somewhere you're not supposed to be?"

"Yeah," said Marissa, watching the bull as it circled behind the man. "Do you?"

"Now, what do you mean by that?" the Jeffrey asked.

Then he heard a snort.

The Jeffrey whimpered, "Eh, ahem . . . hi . . ."

"Marissaaaaaaaa," said Clara, her voice shaky.

"Shh, we'll be fine," said Marissa.

"Help," gulped the Jeffrey.

"Everybody be calm," said Marissa. "Stay still."

"My dress is *red*," said Clara, her voice raspy and scared.

"So is my hair!" whimpered the Jeffrey.

"Bulls hate red!" squeaked Clara.

"That's a myth," said Marissa out of the corner of her mouth. "They can't see color, only—"

The Jeffrey took off running.

"—movement," finished Marissa with a sigh.

The bull's head whipped around, its eyes burning like firebox coals. It lowered its horns. And charged.

"Mommy!" yelled the Jeffrey as he dove to the side and the bull blew past him, narrowly missing him but crushing the bowler hat into the mud. The bull bellowed ferociously as it wheeled around and prepared to charge again.

The train's whistle pierced the air.

"They're leaving!!" squealed Clara. She vaulted over the fence.

Marissa found a gap under the fence and squeezed out. Then she heard a desperate voice cry out "Help!"

Marissa looked back through the fence and saw the bull streaking by, with the Jeffrey on its back, clinging to its horns in sheer terror.

She knew the train was about to leave.

But she couldn't just leave the man there.

She wriggled back under the fence. "Hey, Ferdinand!" she shouted, waving her arms.

"Marissa!" yelled Clara from the other side of the fence.

The bull stopped short, launching the man from its back. The Jeffrey ran away across the field, pants torn open to reveal polka-dot long underwear.

"Let's go!" shouted Clara.

The bull glared.

"It's OK," Marissa said softly, holding up a reassuring hand. "You're OK, Ferdinand."

The bull snorted angrily, and ate a daisy.

"Or not," muttered Marissa.

The bull lowered its head and charged straight at Marissa.

She slipped under the fence just in time, as the bull's horns crashed into the dry wood.

"Now!" shouted Clara as Marissa emerged on the other side.

They sprinted toward the train, where Roosevelt was shaking hands and waving goodbye to his old neighbors. The train released a final whistle blast and began to roll down the tracks. The crowd surged forward. Marissa and Clara became tangled amid the people pushing and shoving. The caboose slipped farther away.

A group of boys broke away and took a shortcut toward a bend in the tracks up ahead. Marissa and Clara followed them, jumping over picket fences and climbing over wagons and troughs. They leapt over a brook and ran across a field as the train rolled around the bend.

The locomotive swept by, trailing smoke and sparks and steam. The baggage car rolled past. Marissa and Clara reached the slope leading to the tracks. The press car went by. They scrambled up the gravel.

The dining car rolled past, and the first-class car. The girls reached the tracks and ran alongside the president's car. Clara stuck out her hand. She reached for the ladder. It was three feet away.

Then two.

Then one.

Then two.

The gap widened.

Three.

The train picked up speed. The ladder moved farther away.

Four feet.

Five.

The president's car swept past Clara's outstretched hand. And so did the caboose. The president was no longer on the back deck. Only Mr. Loeb remained. He looked at Marissa and Clara with a blank expression as the train pulled farther away. He gave a small wave and turned away.

Clara bent over and stopped, but Marissa ran past her and kept running.

"Wait!" Marissa yelled, her throat feeling ragged and cold. "Come back!"

Her breath came in burning gasps and her shoes pounded against the gravel as the roar of the train grew softer. Marissa slowed to a stop, holding her sides. The train whistled in the distance, shrinking into the vast brown-and-yellow grasslands until it became a single dot where the two rails met.

As her breath returned to normal, Marissa said, "We should head back to town."

But no one answered.

Marissa turned and looked back down the tracks toward town.

"Clara!" she yelled, hearing her voice echo across the open plain. A murder of crows took off from the only tree in sight, a spindly oak near the tracks.

"Come on, Clara!" yelled Marissa, scanning the prairie for her sister. "This isn't funny."

The gentle breeze died down. The purple tips of the green-and-yellow grass held still.

"CLARA!" yelled Marissa, hearing her own voice echo across the hard ground. The entire field of grass leaned over in a single movement as the wind picked up again.

A lone rider appeared on the horizon.

CHAPTER 14

KETTLE

MARISSA froze. No place to hide. The rider sped straight toward her on a pale horse that kicked up a haze in its wake. Dust flew from the shoulders of the rider's long, tattered coat, and an old cavalry-style hat hung loosely to the side as he hunched over the reins.

The horse and rider swept past Marissa and wheeled around to face the tracks. The rider was an old man, with a gray mustache and long gray hair. Marissa watched as he dismounted and retrieved a small canteen from a saddlebag that looked as tough as his face.

His eyes were fixed in what looked like a permanent squint. There was a deep scar on his jaw, purple against the red sunburned skin. He spat, blew his nose on a red handkerchief, and stared down the tracks without giving any indication of having noticed Marissa.

Finally the man spoke. He had an Irish accent, with a western edge. "You're waitin' on the Colonel too, then," he said, keeping his eyes on the tracks.

Marissa opened her mouth to speak, but nothing came out. Her throat was dry. Finally she squeaked, "I'm looking for my sister."

The man squinted at her, then looked back down the tracks. "Ain't seen no girls around here. Might try back in town. They'll be gathering for the big man's speech around now, I expect."

"You mean . . . President Roosevelt?" asked Marissa.

The man smiled, revealing a few brown teeth separated by gaps. "He'll always be Colonel Roosevelt to me."

"But he's already gone," Marissa said.

The man's face fell in shock and despair. "NO!" he cried.

"His train left five minutes ago," said Marissa. "We were—" She cut herself off, not sure if she should say any more. The man seemed to have stopped listening anyway, as he pounded the ground with his fist in a tantrum.

"No!!" the man repeated. "No, no, no!" He stood up and threw his hat to the ground in frustration. He looked down the tracks toward town, apparently not believing what he'd just heard. He slowly turned his gaze to the west, where the faint wisps of smoke from the president's train still clung to the air. The man collapsed to the ground. Defeated. He was silent for a moment. Marissa was unsure if she should leave.

The man spoke.

"I chased him up San Juan Hill with the rest of the Rough Riders," he said. "I suppose I can chase him on down the line."

Marissa remembered the faded photograph that hung in the Roosevelt Room, showing Teddy Roosevelt and the Rough Riders at the top of San Juan Hill.

"You were a Rough Rider?" said Marissa.

The man removed a yellow riding glove and pointed at the scar on his cheek. "See that? A kiss from a Spanish bayonet on Kettle Hill." He gestured toward the gray horse. "Named my horse Kettle on account of it."

Marissa stood up and went over to the horse. Instinctively it turned its head toward her and bowed, allowing her to pet it.

"I see you've got a way with horses," said the man.

"Yeah . . ." Marissa eyed the stirrups of the horse. Three years of riding lessons. Two summers of horse camp.

She had to find Clara.

"Sorry," said Marissa as she grabbed the pommel of the saddle and pulled herself on.

"Now, what in—"

"Just borrowing!" Marissa gave Kettle a gentle kick and the horse started to trot alongside the tracks toward town.

"That ain't neighborly!" the man yelled behind them as Kettle grew more comfortable with Marissa and began loping into a smooth gallop.

"I have to find my sister!" Marissa yelled over her shoulder.

A whistle pierced the air and Kettle stopped short, nearly pitching Marissa off the saddle. Marissa regained her position and urged the horse forward. He wouldn't budge. She looked back and saw the man place two fingers in his mouth and whistle again. The horse turned and trotted straight back to him.

"Now then," said the man, firmly grabbing the reins to his horse, "you've misplaced your sister, have you?"

"She was right here!" said Marissa, struggling to maintain her composure.

"The grass is high for this time of year, but not high enough to swallow a child," he mused. "You were out here picking daisies then?"

"We were trying to catch a train!" Marissa said indignantly. "The pres—the Colonel's train. We've been on it all the way from Washington, but then we . . . I . . . made us miss it."

The man took a step back, still holding the reins but looking at Marissa differently. "You're a friend of the Colonel?" he said almost reverently.

Marissa lifted her chin as she said, "We're White House kids."

"You're also a horse thief." He grabbed Marissa by the waist and plunked her heavily on the rear of the horse before swinging himself into the saddle in front of her. "But no friend of the Colonel's gets left to the coyotes on Bill Jones's watch. Let's find your sister."

With Marissa hanging on to his tattered cavalry coat, Bill Jones expertly galloped Kettle up the side of the nearest hill. From here the entire prairie opened up before them—waves of purple heather among golden stalks of grass, with wide patches of trampled green where cattle had eaten their fill. To the east was the town of Medora. To the west were the endless tracks.

"In all my years as sheriff," Jones mused, "I never did have to find a missing child." He looked over his shoulder and glared at Marissa. "I hung a few horse rustlers, though."

Marissa felt a tightness in her throat. She coughed, and tried to sound conversational. "You're the sheriff here?" she asked.

"Used to be," Jones said. "Long time ago. The Colonel was my deputy. And I was his ranch hand. I musta branded the Roosevelt Elkhorn triangle on thousands of cattle. We was like family, him and I. Of course he weren't the Colonel yet, just another New York dandy trying to outrun his troubles by heading west."

They reached the top of the hill. From here they could see the shining steel railroad tracks extending farther into the distance, through the hazy foothills at the end of the prairie.

"Can you imagine?" said Bill Jones, as much to himself as Marissa. "The Colonel's wife died of one thing, mother died of another. Same house, on the same day! It'd be enough to make any man abandon whatever he had left and go chase the sun."

The crows rose and dove again as one over a patch of grassland before circling back to the single oak tree by the tracks, then swiftly taking off once again.

"Where *is* she?" Marissa asked, her stomach churning.

"She'll turn up," Jones said. "Family always comes back, by and by." He straightened up in the saddle and brushed the dust off his sleeve. "The Colonel finally went home to that poor little girl of his, didn't he?"

Marissa barely heard him. She wanted to jump off the horse and run, run as fast as she could, to find Clara.

"I seen her," said Jones.

"Where?" Marissa asked.

"In the papers. They had her picture."

"Clara?"

"No," said Jones. "Ain't you listening?"

"OK," Marissa replied, not listening. She anxiously scanned the horizon again. A light puff of smoke rose in the east. Another train was approaching.

"I'm talking about the little girl the Colonel left behind. Born two days before his wife Alice died."

That caught Marissa's attention.

Jones said, "That little girl was also named—"

"Alice," said Marissa, remembering what Quentin had said about his sister Alice having a different mother.

"That's right. Alice. The Colonel called her his Baby Lee on account of her middle name," said Jones.

"Alice Lee Roosevelt," said Marissa.

"Didn't talk about her much, but he had a little studio photograph of her in his vest pocket. It got all dirty and wrinkled, but he'd show it around still. Now she's all grown up, her picture's in the papers all the time."

"So he . . . he left her behind?" said Marissa, thinking about the baby girl without a mother. Without a father.

"Oh, little Alice did all right," said Jones. "She was with an aunt the whole time, private school and all. And after that blizzard killed off the herd, the Colonel went on back east to his little girl. Family is family."

Marissa looked once more toward the west, letting her eyes take in the horizon, the wide open prairie, the desolate land alongside the tracks, punctuated by a single tree.

The only tree for miles.

"I know where my sister is," said Marissa. She pointed west to the tree.

But Bill Jones had his eyes to the puffs of smoke to the east.

"That must be the freight then," said Jones. "Last westbound of the day, running late behind the Presidential Special." He snapped the reins and said, "Let's get that sister of yours and catch that train!"

Kettle took off running toward the solitary oak tree. In the top branch was a fierce-looking hawk surveying the land, keeping the crows at bay. And a few branches below that was a sullen nine-year-old, leaning against the trunk.

"Clara!" yelled Marissa as they approached.

Clara looked at her. Then turned away in a huff.

Marissa looked behind her and saw the freight train closing toward them.

"This is Bill Jones!" said Marissa. "He's gonna get us on that train so we can catch up to Teddy!"

"What if I don't want to?" said Clara.

"We don't have time for this!" said Marissa.

"We didn't have time to play with the bull either," Clara shouted back.

"That guy was in trouble!" shouted Marissa. "So I decided—"

"Yeah! *You* decided! You always decide!" Clara turned her face to the tree. "And I want to go home!"

"You can't!" Marissa yelled. "This is the last train of the day!"

"Actually," said Jones, taking off his hat, "I said it was the last westbound."

Marissa looked at him. "So there's one heading back east?"

Jones nodded.

Marissa looked up into the tree. Her sister looked away.

"You know what, Clara?" Marissa called over the prairie wind. "You decide. West to California, or east to the White House?"

Clara looked down. "So *now* you want to listen to me?"

"Yes!" shouted Marissa. "Yes, I do! Your turn to make the plans!"

"WELL, I DON'T KNOW!" shouted Clara.

"I DON'T EITHER!" Marissa shouted back.

The train chugged closer. There was a big number 9 on the front of the engine. The ground rumbled and the hawk flew off as the train grew louder.

"Ladies!" yelled Jones over the sound. "East or west?"

"I want to save the tree," Clara said.

"What?" Marissa yelled back.

"I SAID I WANT TO GO WEST AND SAVE YOUR STUPID TREE!" shouted Clara.

"Westward ho!" yelled Jones as the giant locomotive roared past.

Clara scrambled down the tree to the last branch, about ten feet off the ground.

"Go on," Jones yelled, clearing a space in front of the saddle. "Drop to the horse! Kettle can handle the three of us!"

Boxcars rumbled past, shaking the tree. Behind Jones, Marissa shouted, "You can do it!"

"NO I CAN'T!" Clara yelled back.

"She scared of the train?" yelled Jones.

"No!" Marissa yelled back. "She's afraid of your horse!"

"Shut up!" exclaimed Clara as an open car full of iron bars

rolled by, causing the branch to rattle wildly and knocking Clara off balance. She grabbed onto the branch above as her feet slipped. She tried to get her feet back on the lower branch, but she was too far out.

"Come on now," yelled Jones as he guided the horse forward into place below the swinging girl. "Land it like a Rough Rider!"

Clara closed her eyes, released her fingers, and fell onto the horse's shoulders.

"HYAH!" yelled Jones, and the horse bolted forward. Kettle built speed and pulled even with a faded yellow boxcar with a loose handle flapping in the wind. With Clara in front of him clinging desperately to the horse's mane and Marissa behind him clutching his old coat, Jones unhooked a lasso from the saddle and swung it above him in wide circles.

He cracked his wrist and sent the loop flying toward the boxcar. The rope fell short, slapping the rocks beside the tracks.

Jones pulled it back up for another try.

With Kettle's head bobbing up and down and its hooves pounding the rough terrain alongside the tracks, Jones lifted the lasso again, circling it once, twice, three times before releasing it toward the yellow boxcar. This time it caught the flapping handle.

Jones leaned back and the door slid open, revealing a dark boxcar half filled with scattered sacks of grain. He released his grip on the lasso, and the rope tailed off like a long, flowing kite.

Jones urged Kettle forward, pulling in close enough to catch the dust and dirt flying up from the wheels. Jones took Clara by the shoulders and yelled for her to let go of the horse. She didn't

want to. With her fingers tightly gripping the horse's mane and her knees clutching both sides of its neck, she felt safe and alive and did *not* want to get thrown onto a moving train.

But that's exactly what happened. Jones lifted her roughly by the shoulders and tossed her with the same ease he might have tossed one of the sacks of grain she landed on. Turning in a daze, Clara saw her sister fly like a doll into the car as well. As the girls caught their breath and watched in amazement, the old man lifted himself up to a low crouch, with his feet on the saddle of the galloping horse. He released the reins, stood up, and leapt gracefully into the boxcar.

"Whew!" he said, flashing his few brown teeth in a smile.

The girls stared at him, stunned.

"I've spent a minute or two in the saddle," he explained.

"What about your horse?" shouted Clara.

"Kettle knows the way home," said Jones. "I'll meet up with him by and by."

Clara leaned out the open door to look down the tracks, catching a final glimpse as the riderless horse galloped into the rolling hills.

CHAPTER 15

THE TRACKS

AS the freight train chugged west, it always seemed to be going uphill. Scattered pine trees and patches of snow began to replace the brown grassland, but the land remained open and windy. Rain and sleet pelted the boxcar. As Marissa huddled with her sister in the far corner of the car, Bill Jones sat in the opening, getting soaked, with his feet hanging over the edge.

Over the wind and weather, Jones shouted stories about his time as the Billings County sheriff, arresting cattle rustlers and train robbers. "We had one gang, the Miller family. They'd wait for a train to make a water stop," said Jones, "then they'd sneak up in between the cars and pull the pin joining them so when the train started up again, it would leave a car or two behind for the gang to empty out." He laughed. "Then I caught one of the Miller boys with a wagon full of stolen goods and an iron railroad pin in his pocket. And that was that."

The boxcar wheels had a different rhythm from the president's train. Heavier, less cushioned. *Buckle-UP*, Marissa heard every time the wheels cycled forward. *Buckle-UP*. Over and over. *Buckle-UP. Buckle-UP. Buckle-UP.*

"Buckle up!" Marissa remembered her dad shouting that cold day in Minnesota.

It had been the last month of the campaign. Mom was losing the Upper Midwest. Marissa and Clara were missing a lot of school.

Dad brushed bits of ice from his wet overcoat as he settled into the comfortable end of the stretch SUV next to Mom, who was quietly preparing for the next stop.

"It doesn't work!" said Clara, perched on one of the tiny backward-facing jump seats. She yanked in annoyance at the frayed seat belt to her side.

Marissa's seat belt didn't work either, but she draped it over her lap so Dad wouldn't nag. Blinking police lights fragmented the drops of freezing rain on the tinted windows.

Dry, hot air blasted from the vents above Marissa's head.

The little motorcade began to roll away from the community college where Mom had just delivered her third speech of the day. The motorcycles with their riders in rain-streaked ponchos led the way, followed by the lead car. Finally the SUV pulled out, nearly pitching Marissa out of her seat.

"Buckle UP!" said Dad.

"Mom?" said Marissa.

"Your mother's concentrating, mija," said Dad.

"Mom, why do you keep giving the same speech?"

Mom looked up from the thick binder in her lap. "Not now, Mar," she said.

The SUV rocked as it rolled down the rutted dirt driveway.

"It's getting boring," said Marissa, then mimicked her mother's voice: "'I had to stop the highway. I had to get involved' . . ."

"Marissa . . ." Dad said in a warning voice.

"What?" said Marissa, bouncing around on the fragile jump seat as the motorcade picked up speed. "They wanted to build a road through the forest, and Mom ran for office to stop them. Yaaaay!"

"People want to know what motivates her," said Dad.

"People are getting bored," said Marissa.

"Thanks for the vote of confidence," Mom said.

"And that part about 'The forest was my refuge,'" Clara chimed in. "Kinda cheesy, you know? Refuge from what?"

"Mom's parents," answered Marissa.

"That's private," said Dad. "Solo familia."

"It's only family here," said Marissa.

Dad lowered his voice. "We don't want you to talk—"

"I KNOW, DAD!" Marissa said. "You don't want me to talk at all."

"Have a granola bar, sweetie," said Mom without looking up.

"I'm not hungry," growled Marissa. She grabbed a box of honey roasted peanuts from the SUV's little snack bar, tore it open, and ate the whole thing.

"Marissa, you've got to understand we're all under a microscope," said Dad.

"Really?" grumbled Marissa under her breath. "I hadn't noticed."

"Just," said Dad, "keep it together for three more weeks, OK? This will all be over in three weeks."

"But what if we win?" asked Marissa.

"Shadow copy, status bravo," crackled the radio.

"Five minutes," said Dad.

"I know what bravo means," said Mom.

"You ready?" Dad asked.

"Stop asking," Mom responded.

"Girls, leave your mom alone," said Dad.

"What if we win?" Marissa quietly asked again.

Nobody answered. The freezing rain streaked across the purple bulletproof glass.

Buckle-UP buckle-UP buckle-UP buckle-UP

The freight train rumbled over swollen mountain streams and through tunnels carved from rocky hillsides. Jones remained at the doorway, silently regarding the passing landscape, all out of stories to tell.

There were more trees now. Clusters of pine trees thickened into full forests as the train strained up the slope of a mountain.

They looked a lot like the mountains where her mother had grown up. Marissa looked out into the passing forest and tried to picture her mom as a kid, before she grew up and ran for the State Assembly. Before she married a Marine from Long Beach and ran for governor. Before she had kids and ran for president.

But Marissa couldn't picture her mom out there. All she saw were trees.

The girls shivered as the air became colder and thinner. They huddled together on sacks of grain, using Jones's tattered coat as a blanket while he stood in the doorway with his sleeves rolled up.

Jones started talking again, describing the winters of the High Plains. The deep freeze in 1887 that killed off Roosevelt's herd. The sudden and complete whiteout the following year, which they called the Children's Blizzard because of all the schoolchildren who got caught in it on their way home. Some never made it. Marissa shivered and pulled her sister closer.

The train curved around low hills and steep bluffs, thick clouds and swirling snow. The sun broke through and everything cleared as the train chugged into a wide, sunny valley. At the far end was a solid wall of distant jagged peaks, stretching as far as the eye could see.

"The Rockies!" exclaimed Clara.

"Welcome to Wyoming," said Jones.

As the train chased the sun into the mountains, the girls stared at the forests and cliff sides rolling by. A herd of elk galloped alongside the train through a narrow river valley. A single moose stood in the glittering water of a flooded field. As the train strained toward the top of a ridge, the trees turned to little scrubby bushes, then the bushes turned to nothing but snow.

The train crested the ridge, revealing an endless chain of snowcapped mountains reflecting the orange and red of the last rays of sunshine. The massive load picked up speed as the train rolled downhill into the valley beyond, the light dropping into shadows as black trees rose from the dark blue blanket of snow.

When the ground outside leveled out, the train jerked and shuddered. The brakes shrieked against the tremendous momentum, slowing the train to a crawl. Jones held onto the boxcar handle and leaned out for a look.

"Train up ahead!" he yelled to the girls. "Looks fancy!"

Marissa and Clara joined him at the door and peered ahead. In the faint light they saw red-white-and-blue flags hanging from the back of a brightly lit train. "That's it!" said Marissa.

"I'm comin', Colonel!" Jones shouted. "Private Jones reporting for duty!"

"Shh," said Marissa, "we're not exactly welcome."

"Bill Jones is always welcome," said Jones.

The train jerked, skipped, and rattled to a stop. "Come on," said Jones. "The freight train is switching tracks to get around the Colonel. Now's our chance."

Jones hopped off into a snowbank by the side of the tracks and slogged forward. Marissa jumped out after him, feeling the cold snow immediately seep into the cloth shoes on her feet. As they approached the president's train, they saw a campfire surrounded by reporters, laughing and singing. At the edge of the woods stood the other Jeffrey, a short cigar making his mustache glow in the snowy blue moonlight.

Marissa, Clara, and Jones slipped past him and made their way up the side of the train. When Marissa opened the door to the baggage car, she saw a kerosene lantern burning inside.

"Ethel?" asked Marissa.

"Quentin?" asked Clara.

"They're not here," whispered a familiar voice.

The lantern floated toward a familiar face. Alex Lee's eyes glistened.

"Where on earth have you been?" cried the reporter before rushing over and wrapping Marissa and Clara in a tender hug. "Never mind, never mind," whispered Alex Lee. "You're back, and you're safe, that's what matters."

"Where's the Colonel?" asked Jones.

Alex Lee released the girls and said, "The *president* has gone into Yellowstone for a few days of winter camp, with only the park superintendent for company. And who might you be?"

"I might be Bill Jones," said Jones, "lifelong friend of *Colonel* Theodore Roosevelt."

"Bill Jones," the reporter repeated in wonder. "*Sheriff* Bill Jones?"

"If you insist," said Jones.

"I've read all about you," whispered Alex Lee. "In my—I mean in the president's—books about his time out west."

"Never did read 'em," Jones said, "but every word is true."

"So it's true you're an expert tracker?"

"As expert as any, if that's what you're asking."

"You need to find the children," Alex Lee whispered urgently.

"Found two already."

"There's two more," Alex Lee said. "Out in the woods somewhere."

"Quentin?" Clara asked.

"Ethel?" asked Marissa.

"Gone after their father," whispered Alex Lee. "Some silly idea of camping with him."

Marissa remembered their conversation in the clubhouse. More important to the Roosevelt children than saving a tree or sneaking onto a train seemed to be the idea of sharing another campfire with their father, the way they had before he became president.

"If they're with the president, they'll be safe, right?" asked Marissa. "Isn't he supposed to be the king of the woods or something?"

"They're not with him," Alex Lee replied. "They're following him."

"Let's go find them!" exclaimed Marissa, heading for the door.

Jones shook his head. "Can't track them at night. We leave at first light."

First light was an overstatement. When Clara shook Marissa awake the next morning, it was still very dark.

"Bill's outside," she said. "Dress warm."

The girls put on the thickest clothes they could find in Ethel's trunk, along with several pairs of socks, and boots that barely fit.

In the early morning twilight, Jones greeted them with a silent wave on the snowbank running alongside the train. Next to him were three mules, each with a green blanket and a stitched saddle.

Marissa stepped out into the snow and confidently climbed onto one of the mules. Clara crept up to the one that looked the least scary, and Jones helped her into the saddle. He led the girls up a snow-covered hill. When they reached the top, a vast mountain valley opened up in front of them. Pine trees lined the jagged horizon. There were no houses, no roads. The entire valley looked untouched by humans, except for several sets of tracks through the snow.

"That's likely the Colonel," Jones said, pointing to a narrow line through the snow, leading up into the hills straight across from them. "In this depth, the Colonel's horses would've gone single file."

"So what's that?" Marissa asked, pointing to a wider, more pronounced trench leading to the right, following the valley floor. It was pockmarked with large, deep footprints, as well as two sets of much smaller footprints.

"You've got a good eye," said Jones approvingly. "I believe that's where your friends headed."

"They went the wrong way?" asked Marissa, anxiety creeping in.

Jones steered his mule down the valley through the powdery snow. "They didn't follow the Colonel," he said as they approached the trail, "but they mighta thought they were. Something mammoth must of cut a swath like that."

"Mammoth?" Clara asked.

"It means big," said Marissa.

"I know what it *means*!"

"Tracks too wide for a moose . . ." said Jones as they drew closer. He hopped off his mule and examined the trail. "Probably just a bear."

"Just a BEAR?" shrieked Clara.

"So which way?" asked Jones, looking out at the point where the tracks diverged.

"We have to make sure they're OK," said Marissa.

Jones sighed, and nodded. "The Colonel can wait, I s'pose."

"Just a bear," Clara grumbled quietly.

Several quiet hours passed as the girls followed Jones, and he followed the tracks left by Quentin and Ethel. Clara found herself getting used to riding the mule. It seemed tame and slow after her wild ride clinging to Kettle's mane the day before. Clara patted the mule's shoulder encouragingly as it stumbled through melting snowbanks.

"You can do it, Buttercup," she said gently.

"Buttercup?" asked Marissa with a wry smile. Clara ignored her.

The noon sun was surprisingly hot, leading Marissa to regret the many layers she was wearing. Thin streams of water from the melting mountain snow cut across their path and made it more difficult to follow the trail. The trees along the trail became smaller and farther apart. There was less snow here, just exposed stone. And there was a strange, rotten egg smell in the air.

Jones stopped the mules and carefully examined the spare bits of snow, mud, and grass among the rocks, trying to recover the trail. He looked up and shrugged helplessly. "Hey, tree squirrel," he said to Clara, "how's about you put them climbing skills to use and see what you can see?"

He nodded toward a solitary oak tree rising amid the smaller, sickly trees of the stony clearing. Clara dismounted and climbed the tree.

"Oh!" she exclaimed as she neared the top.

"You see them?" asked Marissa.

"No, I see . . ." Clara's voice faded as she looked out on the stony wasteland beyond the trees. There was no snow, only rocks and wide pools of steaming water. Trails of steam slid out of cracks in the rocks, leaving white mineral deposits and rainbow-colored stains on the flat stone surfaces. The smell of rotten eggs was stronger than ever. There was no sign of life.

Until they heard the scream.

CHAPTER 16

THE MILLERS STRIKE AGAIN

"WHAT was that?" Marissa shouted up from the ground.

Clara peered out over the steaming expanse and saw a branch shaking on one of the sparse trees by the clearing. Clara scrambled down her tree and ran toward the movement, with Jones and Marissa close behind. They skirted the edge of the misty clearing and approached the tree, where they could now see two figures climbing upward.

"Quentin!" Clara yelled happily.

"*Shhhh!*" Quentin and Ethel both hissed from the upper branches. Quentin pointed across a smoking crater to a stand of trees on the other side. Among the trees was a massive bear, covered in brown shaggy hair, with a big, muscular neck that rippled with every movement.

"Grizzly," said Jones quietly. "Nothing to worry about, unless she's got—"

Three little bears appeared near the big one.

"—cubs," said Jones.

The big bear stood on her hind legs and waved a threatening paw.

"All right, mama," said Jones softly, "we ain't gonna hurt your babes."

The grizzly bear dropped back to four legs. She took a step forward. The steam seemed to be getting thicker, pouring out of the cracks in the ground.

"Marissa . . ." Clara said in a small, scared voice.

"Shh," Marissa said, gripping her arm.

"Stay still and calm!" a voice boomed from beyond the mist.

Jones peered into the steam. "Who's that there?"

"Steady," said the voice.

Through the cloud of yellow steam they could see the faint shadow of a man in a cavalry hat and a rugged jacket, looking at something in his hand.

"Steady," said the shadow's voice as the bear took several more steps across the smoky ground.

The bear stopped and sniffed the air.

The ground began to shake. The rotten egg smell got worse.

"Steady . . ." said the shadow again, his voice tense.

Jones pulled a knife from his belt as the bear took another step.

"And . . ." the shadow called as the ground shook intensely.

Steam billowed through the cracks.

The bear looked around frantically.

"NOW!" the shadow yelled.

A powerful column of water and steam shot from the center of one of the lakes, sending clouds of heat and sulfur and the scent of rotten eggs into the air.

The grizzly bear scampered backward, startled by the blast. She turned and ran back to her cubs, leading them safely into the woods.

Jones put away his knife and jumped up and down in delight as the hot water fell back to earth. "Old Faithful!" he shouted. "I only heard tell, never seen it with my own eyes."

"Every hour, like clockwork," shouted the shadow.

"Where you at, old man?" yelled Jones.

"My goodness," said the shadow, striding forward. "Is that Hell-Roaring Bill Jones?"

"Reporting for duty, Colonel!" yelled Jones.

The steam faded, revealing the shadow to be Teddy Roosevelt, holding a pocket watch and grinning ear to ear.

The two men ran toward each other and hugged like lost brothers.

"I see you've adopted my stowaways," said Roosevelt with a nod to the girls. "Don't let that little bear worry you," he said to them. "She's not a killer. Not like the cougar that's been stalking this area."

"Cougar?" Clara asked, her voice shaking.

"Oh yes," said Roosevelt. "I've observed several recent kills in the area. Two elk and a deer."

Clara looked toward the path in the woods that led to the spot where they'd left their mules tied to a tree. "Buttercup!" she cried. She broke away and ran down the path.

"What an entertaining young lady," Roosevelt said. "Of course, from the look of the trail I found, there were already two trackers following that cougar by the time I picked up the trace. Greater hunters than I, no doubt."

A branch cracked above them and Roosevelt looked up into the tree. "Now, what . . ."

"Them's your greater hunters up there," said Jones.

Roosevelt squinted at the tree. His mouth dropped. For once, he appeared speechless.

"Hello, Father," said Ethel from one of the branches.

"Good morning, sir," said Quentin from another.

Roosevelt blinked hard, then shook his head. He looked at Marissa with wide, questioning eyes, as if she held all the answers.

Feeling the need to say something, Marissa said, "They missed camping with you."

Roosevelt blinked, nodded, and blinked again. He opened his mouth as if to say something, then closed it. Finally he mumbled, "Please note any interesting birds nests while you're aloft in that tree, children."

Clara arrived back where they'd left the three mules and found the animals still quietly waiting right where they'd left them. She threw her arms around Buttercup's neck. She was still hugging the mule when Marissa and Jones arrived.

"Saddle up!" said Jones. "The Colonel wants us to join his party."

"Will there be . . ." asked Clara nervously.

"Don't be put off by that cougar talk," said Jones. "Them cats only come out at night."

"Oh, that's comforting," said Marissa.

Clara climbed into the saddle of her mule by herself this time. She leaned forward and whispered, "Don't worry, Buttercup, I won't let any mean old cougar bother you."

The girls and their mules followed Jones to a snow-covered clearing where Roosevelt was instructing Ethel and Quentin on the proper way to adjust a saddle. With him was a man with a thin mustache and a uniform cap. This was the park superintendent. He looked at the mules the girls were riding and raised an eyebrow.

"Had to borrow a few mounts," said Jones. "You wouldn't want us trespassing on foot now, would you?"

It was then that Marissa noticed her saddle was branded with a black circle stating *Property of Yellowstone National Park.*

"What was that about hanging horse thieves?" she asked Jones.

"Ain't never hung a *mule* thief," Jones shot back.

Roosevelt shared his horse with his two children, one in front and one in back. Roosevelt and the superintendent took turns in the lead as the horses and mules worked their way through narrow wooded trails and steep mountain passages.

Later that evening, Marissa watched as Roosevelt laughed and swapped war stories with Jones around a crackling campfire. She saw Quentin and Ethel listening to every word. She thought about what Alice had said back at the White House, that her father had forgotten who he was, how he needed to spend some time looking at birds to remember.

An owl hooted in the distance and another answered. A third

joined in the chorus. A log in the fire split, sending a shower of sparks circling up into the starry night sky.

The next morning, they got back on their horses and rode down from the mountains.

"Identify that tree!" Roosevelt ordered Marissa as they rode alongside a large evergreen.

"Uh," said Marissa, "that's a pine tree?"

"Mountain aspen!" shouted Quentin.

"CORRECT!"

"Yeah," said Marissa. "Got it. Hey, um, sir, speaking of trees, can I talk to you about the Steeple Giant?"

"No giants here, child."

"Yes, Mr. President, I know, it's a giant sequoia. In California."

"Take it up with Loeb," said Roosevelt. "He's worked out the details for California."

"Yes, sir," said Marissa, "but—"

"Hold!" said Roosevelt, his palm up in the air. All of the travelers froze. Even the mules seemed to respect his authority. Roosevelt scanned the tree line. A bird tweeted and he smiled. "Remarkable," he whispered.

Ethel looked at Marissa and rolled her eyes.

That evening, as they gathered wood for the campfire, Marissa said, "How are we going get your dad to save the tree?"

"He won't," said Ethel. "We'll save it ourselves."

"Yeah, but he can help, can't he?"

"Maybe," said Ethel, "if we're sneaky enough to make him do it."

After dinner, as they all gathered around the campfire and listened to Roosevelt's stories of the Old West, Ethel said, "Father, when you were my age, did you care about such things as birds, animals, and . . . trees?"

"Certainly!" he said, brightening to the subject. "Had my own little museum of natural history by the time I was your age." He took a sip from his tin cup, stretched out his boots by the fire, and added, "You can start your own museum too, after you return home tomorrow."

"No!" Ethel exclaimed.

"So much for sneaky," muttered Marissa.

"Bill," said Roosevelt, turning to Jones, "when we leave the park tomorrow, I want you to take the children east and see they are returned safely to the White House."

"Colonel," Jones said with a sharp salute, "I promise I'll take your children home!"

Ethel and Marissa exchanged looks of anguish, but there was nothing more they could do. That night, Marissa rested on the pine-covered ground and stared up at the western night sky, searching for constellations and wondering how it was possible to feel so lousy in such a beautiful setting. She closed her eyes.

"Hey, Marissa," whispered Clara.

Marissa wasn't in the mood to talk. She pretended to sleep as she heard Clara move on to talk with Ethel and Quentin.

They returned to the train the next morning, with the smiling president galloping in the lead. His appearance at the train triggered a frenzy of activity as the railroad men scrambled to prepare for departure, and the reporters and dignitaries rushed to the president's horse.

"Did you miss us?" cracked Burns.

"Not in the slightest!" Roosevelt responded. "The farther one gets into the wilderness, the greater is the attraction of its lonely freedom. I've half a mind to quit politics altogether and remain here."

"Aw, we'd miss you too much," said Gordon.

"The feeling is hardly mutual," smiled Roosevelt.

"Wonderful to have you back, Mr. President," said Mr. Loeb in a flat voice as he walked through the snow in dress shoes and a black suit. "I'm afraid we're a bit off schedule, and . . ."

His eyes fell on Marissa and his face pinched in disbelief. Then he saw Ethel and Quentin standing nearby, and he looked as if he might faint.

"Mr. President, what . . . how . . ."

"How indeed," murmured Roosevelt. "No matter. Mr. Jones has it in hand. Isn't that right, Mr. . . ." He looked around, but the mule that had been carrying Bill Jones now stood empty. "JONES!" yelled Roosevelt, his voice triggering a small avalanche of snow from a nearby branch onto Mr. Loeb's neck.

"Right here, Colonel!" Jones responded. He emerged from the shadows between the president's car and the caboose.

"Mr. Jones, I present you with this magnificent horse," Roosevelt said, dismounting from his in a single graceful motion and holding out the reins. "Borrowed," he added, with a nod to the superintendent, "for just as such time as it takes you to convey the children to an eastbound train."

"Of course, Colonel!" said Jones. "I'll take care of your children!"

Jones took the reins from Roosevelt, who smiled, hugged his children, and walked away.

Quentin happily jumped onto the horse.

"How are we all going to fit on that thing?" Marissa asked.

"Not a problem," responded Ethel.

"But what about all our stuff? All those dresses and shoes?"

"It'll be safe on the train," Ethel replied. "Particularly the purple stocking, tucked away behind the lining of my trunk."

"What?" asked Marissa.

"You're always welcome to use my socks."

Marissa stared at Ethel in confusion.

The train whistle released a shriek that echoed across the snow-covered mountains. Mr. Loeb hurried over toward the train.

Then a snowball hit him in the face.

He turned, his face red and wet, cold snow dripping onto his starched white collar and black suit jacket. A second snowball just missed him. Marissa saw a third snowball fly in from the dark space between the president's railroad car and the caboose, just before Clara emerged from the same spot and ran along the side of the train, tucking something into her pocket.

Mr. Loeb's face twisted in rage and he ran after her, losing a shoe in the snow.

"One tree," said Ethel.

"Go on, city girl," Jones said to Marissa, "catch your train!"

"But didn't you—"

"I promised the Colonel I'd take care of *his* kids!" yelled Jones. "And that ain't you!"

Marissa saw her sister climb onto the press car, with Mr. Loeb slipping after her.

The whistle blew again.

"Get in there!" Quentin yelled.

Marissa gave her friends a grateful nod, then ran through the snow, heading for the nearest spot on the train—the gap between the president's car and the caboose. She reached the train and grabbed hold of the iron rail to the side of Roosevelt's car, pulling herself up onto the narrow deck.

The door from the president's car flew open, nearly knocking Marissa off. Clara ran out the doorway.

"Here!" Clara said urgently, shoving a cold piece of metal into Marissa's hand before continuing on into the caboose.

Moments later, Mr. Loeb and the mustached Jeffrey ran by in hot pursuit. As they ran into the caboose, Clara popped out of the cupola window and ran back over the roof. She jumped over the gap onto the roof of the president's car just as the train lurched forward.

But the caboose stayed still.

Marissa stared as the gap widened between the president's car and the caboose.

"The Miller Gang strikes again!" yelled Jones, galloping alongside the train.

Marissa looked down and saw the empty hole where the pin holding the caboose should have been. Marissa looked back up at the caboose getting smaller in the distance. She looked down at her own hand, at the item Clara had handed her when she went running by. It was a black iron railroad pin.

A shrinking Mr. Loeb appeared in the caboose doorway. A shrinking Wendell hopped up and down at his side, waving his little arms, shouting himself hoarse. Mr. Loeb stood perfectly still, staring openmouthed as the president's train left him behind.

Marissa heard a clunk. She turned and saw Clara, triumphantly climbing off the ladder from the president's roof. She casually took the pin back from Marissa, gave Mr. Loeb a small wave, and turned away.

CHAPTER 17

ALEX LEE

"ARE you crazy?" Marissa yelled over the roaring clatter at what was now the back of the train. She held on tightly to the railing on the narrow metal deck, watching the caboose fade into a little red blur. "This is crazy!"

"We knew you'd say that!" Clara yelled back.

"We?"

"I tried to tell you last night," yelled Clara, her hair whipping wildly in the wind, "but you were pretending to sleep."

"Oh come on—"

"And Ethel said you'd play your part best if you didn't know."

"Did she really?"

"She was right!" Clara grinned, showing her missing teeth. "You kept Loeb distracted right when we needed it! You're the *best*!"

"You're a twerp!" Marissa shouted.

"I know, right?" Clara yelled back.

The train was at full speed now, and the snow-tipped evergreens of Yellowstone flew past quick enough to form a single blurry wall of green.

One tree.

That was the last thing Ethel had said to her.

One tree.

They'd made it across the country. They'd given the Roosevelt kids a chance to reconnect with their father by the light of a campfire. They'd awakened something in the president, changed the way he talked, maybe even changed the way he thought. Reminded him of who he really was.

But the mission remained. Saving one tree. One of the last of its kind. Marissa was determined to see this through. She knew it in her bones. Their work wasn't yet done.

Without Mr. Loeb or the Jeffreys to worry about, Marissa and Clara helped themselves to a white-tablecloth meal. They filled their plates with generous slabs of pot roast and mashed potatoes and green beans and carrots and hot toasted rolls.

"Quentin would have loved this," Clara said with a mouthful of mashed potatoes.

"Yeah," said Marissa. "Ethel too."

One tree.

But how?

Marissa shoved a forkful of pot roast into her mouth. "We're on our own now," she said, looking down at her plate, as much to herself as her sister. But it wasn't her sister who replied.

"White House kids are never alone," whispered a familiar voice.

Marissa's head jerked up. A brown hat rose into view from the next booth over. Alex Lee stood and walked past the girls.

"Wait, what?"

Marissa dropped her fork and chased after the reporter. But as Marissa reached the end of the dining car, Phillips and Burns busted through from the opposite direction.

"Hey, it's the lost princess!" Phillips said with a smile.

"Ready for more cards?" asked Burns.

Marissa ignored them and pushed forward, chasing the reporter in the brown hat. "Alex!"

Marissa finally reached the press car, but the corridor was empty. She ran the length of the corridor, breathlessly bursting into the farthest compartment.

Gordon snored in a corner with a newspaper on his face, but Alex Lee wasn't in the compartment. Marissa saw the reporter's brown leather bag on the floor by the window. She knelt beside it and began searching through the books and notebooks inside.

"Er," said Gordon sleepily, looking over his newspaper, "figure you maybe should leave that alone?"

"Where's Alex?" demanded Marissa.

"I'm not that kid's keeper," Gordon grumbled. He pulled the newspaper back over his face and began snoring again.

Marissa pulled several books out of Alex Lee's bag. Each was a book about the West by Theodore Roosevelt, and all three looked well read and heavily marked up. Marissa dug farther into the bag. Her fingers brushed against something cold. Bumpy. And moving.

Marissa dropped the bag and it fell on its side. Pencils and notebooks scattered across the floor, along with a little toy leather horse and a small, green, live snake. It wriggled furiously on the floor and disappeared under the bench.

"Marissa!" exclaimed Clara from the door of the compartment. "Why'd you run off like that?" She entered the compartment and sat down, looking at the toppled bag.

Marissa kept staring at the spot where the snake had disappeared. Then her eyes shifted to the toy horse. The one Alex had tried to hide the first time they'd met. The one with the black triangle on its flank.

"Marissa?" Clara ask uncertainly, kneeling next to her sister. "Why were you digging through Alex Lee's stuff?"

Marissa picked up the little toy horse. She felt someone watching her from the doorway of the compartment. She turned and saw the toy horse's owner, staring at her from beneath a brown hat.

"This stuff isn't Alex Lee's," said Marissa, looking at the eyes beneath the brim of the hat. "It's Alice Lee's."

The brown hat nodded slowly. Then a gloved hand reached up, took hold of the brim of the hat, and pulled it away, revealing long auburn hair, tucked into a bun.

"Whaaaaa?" said Clara, completely confused.

"Alice Lee Roosevelt," said Marissa.

"We should hardly be so formal," said Alice in a clear, direct voice, stepping into the compartment and sliding the door shut behind her. "If we start using middle names around here, you'll have me at a disadvantage because I don't know yours."

"Alice," Clara asked, "what are you doing here?"

Alice turned and fixed a gaze on the girl. "I could certainly ask you the same question, now couldn't I?" She fixed the hat back on

her head, resuming her disguise as Alex Lee. "When I overheard you all cooking up this madness," she said, "I decided I must ride along to keep an eye on you."

"I *knew* I heard somebody outside the clubhouse!" Marissa said. "That was *you*!"

"Why, of course it was me," said Alice briskly, "it's always me."

"But how . . ." asked Clara.

"Oh, I know how the entire White House functions, my dear," said Alice. "I can balance on a slide and spy on you. I can also write a press credential and secure a seat on the train for 'Alex Lee.' And it's not like this is the first time I've donned a man's outfit to sneak out of the White House."

Gordon's snoring came to a sputtering halt in the corner of the compartment. "There a woman talking here?" he mumbled beneath the newspaper on his face.

"No," Alice said in the raspy whisper of Alex Lee. "You're just having a crazy dream."

"Crazy dream," Gordon agreed sleepily.

"Good night, Gordon," said Clara.

"Night night," Gordon sighed, and drifted back off to sleep.

Alice sat down next to Marissa and removed her leather gloves. She took the toy horse and held it in her finely manicured hand.

"Father gave this to me," she said quietly, "when I was younger. When he worked at the Navy Yard, me and little Ted and Kermit— it was only us three then—we would wait for the streetcar to take him home. Sometimes he'd bring home little gifts."

Clara sat on the other side of Alice and reached curiously for the horse. But Alice clutched it like a small child unwilling to share.

"There," said Alice quietly, running her thumb over the triangle on the flank of the toy horse. "I branded that myself. Father showed me how. With a hot needle."

"The Elkhorn triangle," said Marissa.

"That's right," said Alice.

"Bill Jones told me," said Marissa.

"Ah yes," said Alice. "*Sheriff* Bill Jones."

"He knew a lot about you."

"That's not uncommon," said Alice. "I'm quite famous."

"No, I mean," said Marissa, "when you were little. Your dad told him all about you."

Alice let the hand holding the toy horse fall to her lap and she turned to Marissa, eyes suddenly hard. "That, I find hard to believe."

"Why?" asked Clara.

"Because my father ran away west to forget about me."

Marissa and Clara exchanged looks.

Outside the window, the forest thinned. A broad stream gurgled alongside the train.

Alice let out a deep breath and clutched the horse. "Actually, he ran to forget my mother. And it would appear he succeeded."

"Come on," Marissa blurted, "you can't—"

"Oh can't I? Have you ever heard Father mention my mother by name?" asked Alice. "Good gracious, he doesn't even call *me* by that name. To him, I'm not Alice, I'm Baby Lee."

"That's a nice nickname," said Clara.

"See any mention of me," Alice continued, "in those books he wrote while playing around out west? See any pictures of my mother in the White House?"

"We didn't really spend much time—"

"He ripped her out of his memory!" exclaimed Alice. "Put an X in his diary. Bolted west and abandoned every reminder of her. And me."

"Not every reminder," said Marissa.

Alice scowled. "Don't speak of things you know nothing about."

"Bill saw your picture," said Marissa.

Alice regarded Marissa with a sidelong stare and said, "Everybody's seen my picture."

"I mean, your baby picture," said Marissa. "He said it was all worn and bent, from your father's vest pocket."

"Baby picture?" said Alice in a small voice Marissa hadn't heard before.

"That's what Bill said."

Alice sat back against the seat. She turned away from the girls, holding a hand up to the side of her face as she watched a glistening pond roll past the window.

"Honestly," said Alice, her voice quivering and small, "I never knew he even thought of me back then." She took a deep breath and wiped her eye. She looked down at the toy horse in her hand.

For a while, no one said anything. Gordon snored, and the train rattled on.

"I used to play with this," Alice finally said, voice steady, eyes far away. She stroked the little fur mane of the toy horse. "I'd dream of coming out here to his beloved West, just to breathe the same air that he used to breathe."

"So that's really why you're here," said Marissa.

Alice seemed to nod slightly. Then her look hardened and she faced Marissa.

"No," she said, "that would be foolish," her confident and businesslike tone returning. "I'm here to keep you two out of trouble."

"Yeah, but you've got all those books . . ."

"One must read something on long train rides," Alice replied. "Just to pass the time."

Marissa watched Alice watching the window. The train cut through a gap in the ridge, thick with giant pines. Alice's reflection shone faintly on the glass against the passing trees, her eyes staring, searching.

"Loeb!" bellowed the voice of Teddy Roosevelt from the corridor outside the closed compartment door.

Gordon startled awake and pushed the newspaper from his face. Alice shoved the toy horse into her bag and pulled the hat firmly over her eyes.

Through the thin compartment wall separating them from the poker game next door, they heard Roosevelt shout, "Where's Loeb!"

"He ain't been through here," said Clement's voice. "We'da noticed."

"Well, it seems no one has yet noticed that we've LOST AN ENTIRE TRAIN CAR," fumed the president's voice. "I opened the door from my car and nearly fell out onto the tracks FOR LACK OF A CABOOSE!"

Gordon looked at Alice and the girls with wide eyes. Through the wall they could hear the reporters coughing and sputtering, trying not to laugh.

"Yes, yes, funny for all of you, I should think," said Roosevelt. "Will you keep laughing when the trip goes off center because my right-hand man isn't here to manage the details? If Loeb is gone, there's no one left on this train who understands how things work!"

Marissa looked at Alice. Alice looked down.

"Well," said Roosevelt, "if by some miracle Mr. Loeb does appear, would you please tell him I'm taking lunch with the senators in my car?"

"Yes, Mr. President," said Clement's voice.

"Good day, gentlemen," said Roosevelt's voice, sounding more distant as he headed down the corridor. "I suppose I'll have to go order my own lunch."

Gordon grinned in amazement. He stood up and bolted for the poker compartment. The girls were alone with Alice.

"You have to tell your dad you're here!" said Marissa. "You heard him—he needs someone who understands how things work!"

Alice shook her head. "No, no, no," she said.

"Didn't you say you know how the entire White House functions? Your father needs you!" urged Marissa.

Alice shook her head again and pulled a book out of her bag, turning her back to Marissa and starting to read.

"OK, fine, if you don't care if your father needs you, how about the president? The president needs you. Which means the country needs you. Isn't that what all this clubhouse junk is supposed to be about?"

"It's not my place," murmured Alice, pretending to concentrate on the book.

"Suddenly you care about staying in your place?" asked Marissa.

She felt something brush against her ankle. A moment later she saw Clara raise her feet and go pale with fear. Marissa knew immediately what it was.

"Alice," Marissa said, "I think your . . ." Then she stopped. She dropped down on her hands and knees.

"What are you on about now?" asked Alice, keeping her eyes fixed on her book.

Marissa reached under the seat and felt around near where Clara had jerked her feet up. Marissa's fingers touched cold scales. She grabbed the snake that was hiding there and quickly stood up. She opened the compartment door and ran out into the corridor.

"Hey!" Alice said, noticing her snake being kidnapped. "Stop!" she said, chasing Marissa into the corridor and forgetting to disguise her voice. Several reporters looked out of the poker compartment in surprise as Alice tried to cover for her mistake by saying "Stop" again in a lower voice.

Marissa ran out of the press car and into the dining car. She saw one of the chefs place a round silver dome on a serving tray full of beef and vegetables. Marissa grabbed the tray and said, "I got this!"

Marissa tried her best to keep the tray steady as she ran through from the dining car into the first-class car, past the cigar-smoking congressmen and businessmen, and on to the door at the end leading to the president's car. She placed the silver domed tray on the bench outside the president's door and knocked loudly, then turned back into the first-class car and crashed right into Alice.

"Give me back my snake!" Alice yelled over the noise from the open door.

Marissa smiled and raised her empty hands.

Alice reached into Marissa's pockets and found nothing. "Where is Emily Spinach?" Alice demanded.

Then her face dropped as she looked over Marissa's shoulder and saw her father open his door and carry the tray into his private car.

Alice pushed past Marissa and pulled open the president's door. She saw her father seated at a table between two men in expensive suits, one with silver hair and the other with white hair.

Roosevelt had his hand on the round silver dome. Before Alice could speak, he lifted it.

"AH!" cried the white-haired man.

"SNAKE!" shouted the silver-haired man.

Both men jumped out of their seats. The silver-haired man stood on his chair while the white-haired man ran around in panicked circles. Roosevelt remained seated and still. He held the silver dome in his hand, regarding the little green snake on the platter with a calm face.

"Senators," Roosevelt said quietly, "I believe you know my daughter Alice."

The senators stared at Alice in disbelief. The chugging of the train was the only sound.

Finally the white-haired senator coughed and said, "Lovely to see you, miss."

The silver-haired senator turned to Roosevelt. "Mr. President, how could your daughter—"

"Senator Mattoon," Roosevelt responded wearily, "I can be president of the United States, or I can control Alice. I cannot possibly do both." He put the dome to the side and cradled the snake in his hand, allowing it to slither between his fingers. "Gentlemen, perhaps we should lunch another day."

"Of course," said Senator Mattoon.

"Happy to oblige, Mr. President," said the other man.

The senators slipped past Alice and Marissa and escaped the president's car as if it were on fire. Roosevelt put the snake down, wiped his wire-rimmed eyeglasses, and sighed. "What am I going to do with you, Alice?"

The whistle blew and the train began to slow.

Alice snapped into action. "You're going to ask me to help you prepare for your arrival in Cheyenne."

She walked over and sat down at his table. "Now, according to your book, the last time you were in Cheyenne was . . ."

Marissa opened the door behind her and slipped out, leaving Roosevelt and Alice to figure out how to handle the next stop on their journey.

CHAPTER 18

CHANGE THE MATH

AS the president's train headed west, Roosevelt was barely ever seen without Alice at his side. She offered advice, talked through upcoming speeches, and handled the details of the trip.

As Alice had predicted at the White House, Roosevelt seemed to become more relaxed as the train moved farther west. When a little girl at one of the stops gave him a baby badger named Josiah, Roosevelt accepted the gift with a delighted grin and held the sharp-clawed creature throughout his speech.

Marissa had a hard time imagining Mr. Loeb ever letting something like that happen. But Alice just stood out of the way, letting her father be himself. Then she made sure the badger was locked away in the baggage car.

"It's a rug with teeth," said Clara, watching from a wary distance as Marissa fed the animal bread and milk through the wooden bars of its cage.

"Don't listen to her," Marissa whispered to the badger. "You're a little sweetie, aren't you, Josiah?"

"Why doesn't Alice take care of it herself?" asked Clara.

"She's kinda busy running the country," said Marissa.

"Too busy for us, that's for sure," said Clara.

"That's all right," said Marissa, breaking up another loaf of bread for Josiah. "I just wish we could talk to her about the tree."

"Why?" asked Clara. "We've got it covered!"

Marissa sat up and looked at her sister. "How's that?" she asked. Josiah grunted impatiently and Marissa crouched back down to feed him more bread.

"We stick to the plan," replied Clara.

"We don't have a plan."

"Sure we do," said Clara. "What Quentin said in the clubhouse. Climb the tree and refuse to get out when they try to cut it down."

"Yeah, well, Quentin's not here anymore."

"So I'll do it," said Clara. "I'm a better climber than him anyway."

"Sure," said Marissa, "and unlike Quentin, you've actually seen a giant sequoia. So you know they don't have any low branches!"

"I can climb anything," Clara responded.

"And then what?" asked Marissa. "Stay up there forever?"

"I can stay up there for a hundred years and not even be born yet," replied Clara.

That statement tied Marissa up in enough knots that she decided to let the matter drop. But with every passing stop, her anxiety grew. Finally Marissa managed to catch Alice alone in the corridor of the press car.

"Alice," Marissa said, "you have to talk your dad into saving the Steeple Giant."

Alice gave Marissa an amused smile, then started walking away toward the dining car.

"It's"—Marissa chased after her—"it's a tree. Super old. It's—"

"I'm well aware of the tree of which you speak," said Alice. "And the political winds are blowing smack into it. Unless you can change the math, the valley must flood."

Marissa stopped, stunned, as Alice kept walking.

"But," Marissa cried, "but you can't let that happen! You gotta help us!"

"You *have got to*," Alice corrected her, enunciating each syllable. "Hmm, still sounds a bit undignified—why not just say 'You must'?"

"OK, you *must* help us," said Marissa.

"Must I?" Alice said, turning with a raised eyebrow. "So demanding you've become." She raised a finger. "However, I believe I understand. It was you who put me in a position of power on this train. And so now here you are demanding a favor in return."

"No, I—"

"Oh, I don't mind being used," said Alice. "In fact, I quite admire it. You seem to have become quite the expert in the ways of politics."

"I'm not using . . ." stammered Marissa.

"Frankly, I've always been drawn to the cutthroat over the meek," said Alice. "So much more interesting. If you haven't got anything nice to say, come sit by me, I always say."

"Stop it, Alice!" Marissa yelled in frustration. "I thought you were supposed to help our mission!"

"Do you think your mission is the only thing of importance?"

"Well, no . . ." said Marissa.

"Do you understand that my father faces an election in just eighteen months?"

"But we can't go home unless—"

"What do you care more about," Alice asked, "saving your tree or getting home?"

"I mean . . ."

"What if I were to tell you there's a simple switch in that clubhouse that would open any door? One that could take you home without obliging you to save the tree?"

"There is?" Marissa asked eagerly. "Where?"

Alice regarded her thoughtfully and said, "That's what I thought." She turned and walked through the door.

"Hey," said Marissa, following her inside the packed dining car. "That wasn't fair."

Alice ignored her and smiled brightly at a curly-haired man with a flowing goatee. "*Mr.* Rigby Jr.," she said, shaking his hand. "Dee-lightful to see you this evening, I hope all is well at your bank!" she exclaimed.

"It's Father's bank," said Rigby Jr. with an embarrassed smile. "I am merely an employee."

"Oh, don't be so modest," Alice said.

She moved on to the next table and shook the hands of Gordon and Burns, then moved to another table and chatted happily with several businessmen sporting red carnations in their lapels.

When they left the dining car, Marissa turned and pointed an accusing finger at Alice. "There's no switch in the clubhouse, is there?" The train rattled and shook. "You were bluffing me, just to get me to say—"

Alice laughed and said, "Look how much she knows about poker already!" Then she said, "Whether or not there is a switch, my dear, you've shown your cards. You'd throw that tree over in a heartbeat if it weren't for this supposed mission, wouldn't you?"

"No!" protested Marissa. "It's not just the mission. We have to save that tree. It's important, 'cause it's, it's . . ."

"Old?" asked Alice.

"Ancient!" Marissa responded. "And . . . and . . . wise! I mean, OK, that sounds stupid, but—"

"Frankly, that's the first sensible thing you've said all day," said Alice. "You're starting to make me think you honestly care."

"I do!"

"Which is handy," said Alice, "because the first step in making others care about something is to care about it yourself."

Alice turned and walked into the first-class car. "Senator Mattoon!" Alice exclaimed gleefully as she encountered the silver-haired man smoking a cigar. "And how *is* the gentleman from California?" asked Alice.

"Splendid, Miss Roosevelt, just splendid!" Senator Mattoon replied. "And how is your father?" he asked.

"Looking forward to visiting your state, of course," said Alice.

"Please tell him I appreciate his commitment to the Wendell Dam," said Senator Mattoon.

Marissa scowled, but Alice smiled broadly. "The president is ever mindful of the Golden State's many people and industries."

"And its delegates for his reelection, I expect," chortled Senator Mattoon.

Alice laughed right along with him, then proceeded down the first-class corridor, shaking hands with nearly a dozen other men. Marissa pushed through the crowd and reached her just as she was about to head into the president's car.

"So can you talk to him?" pleaded Marissa as the train rattled over a bridge. "Please tell him to save that tree!"

"Oh, certainly," shouted Alice over the noise, her auburn hair whipping in the wind. "I'll just say, 'Father, you need to stop a major project that all of your allies in California want because a time-traveling trespasser crawled out of your wall and said please.'"

"So that's a no?"

"You need to change the math," Alice said.

"What does that even mean?" Marissa asked.

Alice shook her head, annoyed. "Did you notice nothing from our walk down the train?"

"Um," said Marissa.

"Bankers. Newspapermen. Senators. Why do you think my father invites all of these people on his train?" Alice asked. "You think he just wants to have them all out for a picnic?"

"No . . ." said Marissa.

"He wants to convince them of things, gain their support, influence them," said Alice. "And they want to do the same thing to him! So now it's your turn. Change the math so the votes, the money, and the press are all on your side, not the side that wants to drown your tree!"

She opened the door to her father's car and walked inside, turning back to add, "That's politics!"

Change the math, Marissa thought as she walked back into the first-class car. How do you change the math when everyone is against you?

"Excuse me, young lady," said a voice behind her. She turned to see Senator Mattoon emerging from the first-class car. "Is the president available?"

"Oh, I don't . . ." mumbled Marissa, "I mean, I'm not sure . . ."

The senator nodded politely, then made his way around her toward the door of the president's car. Marissa wondered what Roosevelt thought of this senator. Was he one of the "cold and timid souls" he'd said were infesting the train? The ones who never took chances, who "neither knew victory nor defeat"?

Or could that describe herself?

Get in the arena, Marissa thought. Change the math.

"I wouldn't go in there if I were you," she said.

The senator had his fingers on the president's door handle, but he stopped. "Well, I merely want to offer some friendly advice . . ."

"His best adviser is in there already," said Marissa. "Something I can help you with?"

"Boring old politics," said the senator with a smile. "You wouldn't understand."

"Mm. Yeah. OK," said Marissa.

She made her way through the train, mostly empty now as all the guests were out on the platform. All except the young banker, Rigby Jr., who was sitting alone in the dining car finishing off a strawberry shortcake with a cup of black tea.

"You're not out listening to the president?" he asked when he saw Marissa.

Marissa shrugged, walked up to the buffet, and cut herself a slice of chocolate layer cake.

"I've seen him speak before," she said.

Rigby Jr. smiled. "So have I." He lowered his voice and said, "Honestly, I'm more fascinated by the landscape out here than the speechmaking. Perhaps I'll turn in early so I don't miss the sunrise."

Marissa looked over at him. Change the math, she thought. She poured herself a glass of milk. "Can I join you?" she asked.

"Why, certainly!" Rigby Jr. said brightly. "You know, I have three children, right about your age, back home in Philadelphia."

"Cool," said Marissa, sitting across from him and taking a bite of her cake. "They ever been out west?"

"No," said Rigby Jr. sadly. He sipped his tea. "Someday I will bring them here. They would love the wilderness."

"What if the wilderness is gone by then?" Marissa asked.

"Oh, I highly doubt—"

"You know anything about the Wendell Dam?"

"Of course!" said the young banker proudly. "The Rigby Bank—my employer—is a primary financier of the project."

"Bummer," said Marissa.

"Pardon?"

"Nothing," said Marissa. She picked up her plate and stood up. "It's just your bank is gonna drown a two-thousand-year-old tree. Bet your kids would have liked to see it, but I guess if they wait another two thousand years . . ."

Rigby Jr. laughed nervously. "Well, surely . . ."

"Nice talking to you," said Marissa.

"Now wait, perhaps . . ." stammered the man as Marissa left the dining car with a slight smile on her face. Maybe she could play this game after all.

CHAPTER 19

THE TELEGRAM

THE next morning, Marissa went to the press car and slipped into the first compartment.

Change the math, she thought to herself. Change the math.

Gordon returned to the compartment with a few flecks of shaving cream stuck to his cheeks. He walked over to his briefcase and pulled out a wallet.

Then, without looking at Marissa, he muttered, "You again, eh?"

"Don't you want to write about something more interesting than rich people dancing on dead trees?" asked Marissa.

"Whatever pays the bills, my friend," said Gordon. He headed for the door.

"Isn't it a little early for cards?" asked Marissa.

"Never too early for cards," he replied.

"I have a story for you," said Marissa. She tossed the folder onto Gordon's empty seat.

He turned and looked at the folder. "What's that?" he asked.

"Oh, just a little something out of Mr. Loeb's files."

"That's espionage, kiddo."

"Mm."

"Spying."

"I know what espionage means."

Gordon looked down at the folder again. He sat down and started peeling through the pages regarding plans for the Wendell Sierra Power Network.

"'Cut what we can, burn what we can't, blast what's left,'" Gordon read the telegram out loud. "Not the best foot forward."

"And look," Marissa said, opening the map and showing the many planned lakes along the range and all of the expected development surrounding them. "There won't be any trees left!"

"Come on," said Gordon. "There will always be trees."

"Not the big ones," said Marissa.

"Is that the big story you promised me?" asked Gordon with a wry smile. "Stop the presses! Smaller trees!"

Marissa took the folder back. "You don't think this is worth reporting?"

"What I think doesn't matter," he said. "I wire it in, my editor decides what goes on the front page. And this"—he held his hands open in a helpless gesture—"there's just no front page here."

"What page would it go on?" asked Marissa.

Gordon smiled. "It would go right on top of the 'Things That Make Kids Sad' section."

Sad kids. More like mad kids, thought Marissa. But she wasn't mad at Gordon. She was mad at Wendell. She was mad at Mr.

Loeb. She was mad at Rigby Jr. . . . no. He was nice. Even if his bank was providing the money. Maybe . . .

Marissa stood up. "Don't worry, Gordon, I'll get you a story."

"What do you have up your sleeve?" he asked.

"Gordon!" Clement yelled again through the wall. "It's your deal!"

"They only want me there because they know I'll lose money to them," Gordon said.

"You pick your nose when you have bad cards," said Marissa.

"Who told you that?"

"One of the little girls who stole your lunch money," said Marissa.

She hurried down the corridor toward the dining car, where she saw Rigby Jr., transfixed by the wide desert of Nevada, punctuated by cliffs striped with magenta-and-copper-colored rock. His hands moved rapidly over a small sketch pad.

Marissa plopped down across from Rigby Jr. and said, "Remember that two-thousand-year-old tree your kids won't ever get to see?"

Rigby Jr. blinked and turned his face from the window. "Good morning," he said.

"I figured out how you can save it," said Marissa.

"Oh?"

"Stop giving them money," said Marissa.

Rigby Jr.'s lips turned up in a small smile, and he returned to his sketching. "If only it were that simple," he said sadly.

"It *is* that simple," said Marissa. She opened the folder and spread the map out on the table. "Wendell is gonna knock down every big tree forest in the Sierras. How's he going to get the money to do that?"

"Well, there are a variety of financial instruments available—"

"You're giving him the cash!"

"Not me personally," Rigby Jr. stammered. "I have a fiduciary responsibility to—"

"Why do adults use big words when they don't have a real answer?" asked Marissa.

Then another voice said, "Ah, the grand plan!"

Marissa and Rigby Jr. both looked up to see Senator Mattoon, leaning over the table and viewing the markings on the map with enthusiasm.

"Exciting things, yes?" the senator asked. "The future of the Golden State!"

Gordon and Burns entered and attacked the steaming breakfast buffet, carrying plates piled high with hot slabs of bacon, thick pancakes, and scrambled eggs to an empty table.

"Senator," Marissa asked innocently, "since, as you said, children can't understand boring old politics, I was wondering if you might be able to help me understand something."

"Certainly," Senator Mattoon said, reaching over to the buffet for a cinnamon roll.

Clara walked into the car and helped herself to a heaping pile of pancakes with powdered sugar and too much syrup.

"Senator, I'm just wondering," asked Marissa, "is making thousands of kids cry considered good politics, or bad politics?"

Two tables away, Burns giggled into his orange juice.

Senator Mattoon looked down at his cinnamon roll. "I'm sorry," he said, "I must have misheard."

"Crying children," said Marissa. "Good or bad?"

"Sometimes, my dear," said Senator Mattoon, "progress demands . . ."

Gordon took out a small notebook and started scribbling. "'Crying Kids Sometimes Good, says Senator.'"

"That is most certainly not what I said," sputtered Senator Mattoon.

Rigby Jr. said, "I want it noted that the Rigby Bank does not—"

"It's immaterial," said Senator Mattoon, his face turning red. "There are *no crying children*!"

Marissa looked at Clara, seated alone with syrup covering her mouth. Clara got the hint and began to sob, loudly.

"'Senator Makes Kid Cry,'" Gordon said as he wrote more notes.

"Let me state for the record," said Rigby Jr., "that the Rigby Bank would never cause children distress."

"So you're rethinking the dam?" asked Marissa.

"You're rethinking the dam?" Senator Mattoon asked.

"'Bank Rethinks Dam,'" Gordon murmured as he wrote.

"No, no," stammered Rigby Jr., "the project will continue—"

"'Bank Rethinks Rethinking Dam,'" Gordon muttered.

Clara threw her head back and wailed even louder.

"*However*," Rigby Jr. said defensively, "perhaps we must reexamine the *future* projects for their impact and viability—"

"But, but," Senator Mattoon sputtered desperately, "you can't!"

"'Bank Makes Senator Cry,'" announced Gordon.

"Well, no," Rigby Jr. huffed, "I simply mean that on a case-by-case basis—"

"So you're still gonna drown the tree," said Marissa.

"The project is well underway!" cried Rigby Jr. as he stood and headed toward the door of the dining car.

"That's what you're gonna tell your children?" Marissa asked as he went by.

"Could you please stop talking?" asked Senator Mattoon as he chased after Rigby Jr.

A familiar voice spoke from behind a newspaper at the farthest table. "Remind me not to get on your bad side."

"Just changing the math, Alice," said Marissa.

The newspaper lowered. "Admirable," said Alice. "But here's one more piece of math: There's only one stop before we get to California. You're running out of time for politics."

"CAR-son City, Ne-VA-da!" yelled the conductor.

"Time for direct action," Alice said as she left the car.

At the other end of the car, Clara was giving an Oscar-worthy performance, telling Gordon how much she needed the big tree saved. Big tears rolled down her cheeks as Gordon eagerly scribbled every word in his notebook.

Marissa gathered her papers from the table where Rigby Jr. had been sitting. She opened Wendell's California power map and found

Carson City, just over the Nevada border on the shores of Lake Tahoe. She traced her finger along a rail line leading into the Sierras on the California side, and spotted a station marked Raymond, California. The town was as close as the train would get to the Steeple Giant— about an inch away on the map. From there, the train line swerved up and over on its course toward San Francisco.

Marissa looked again at the place where the Steeple Giant was marked. There was a little pencil mark next to it that she hadn't noticed before. It was a date.

Tomorrow's date.

The train jerked to a stop and Gordon appeared at Marissa's side.

"Can I borrow this stuff?" he asked, quickly folding the map and stuffing the rest of the papers into the folder. "You delivered, kid," he said. "These files plus that stuff with the bank and the senator, topped off by an interview with a crying child—now *that's* a story."

With that he headed off onto the platform. Through the window, Marissa saw him run straight to the Western Union telegraph office. He was going to telegraph an article in to his San Francisco paper for the next edition.

But would that be enough? Or was it all too little, too late?

"Hey, Clara," said Marissa.

"Wasn't I awesome?" Clara asked with her mouth half full of bacon. "Did you see the waterfalls I made on my face?"

"Clara, you're right," said Marissa. "We don't have time for my way anymore. I think they're gonna cut it down tomorrow. So we have to get out there and stop them."

Clara chewed thoughtfully on her bacon.

"I mean, don't you think so?" asked Marissa. "Like maybe we can get the newspapers to talk about the tree and get the voters to rise up and protect it and get the bank to stop paying for it, but all that's going to take time, and that's something we don't have, so we have to take action, you know?"

Clara nodded, tapped her chin, then said, "Sorry, I kinda blanked out on everything you said after 'Clara, you're right.' But yeah, sure."

When the train was underway again, Marissa retrieved the papers from Gordon, who showed her the story he'd sent in to the afternoon paper, headlined "Schoolchildren Roiled by Industry Baron's Scheme, Bank Ponders Retreat."

Marissa and Clara raided the dining car for as much food as they could carry, and assembled bundles of clothes to take with them off the train in Raymond. As the train climbed high into the pine-covered mountains, they dug through the trunks and the piles of clothes to make sure they weren't forgetting anything.

"Marissa?" asked Clara, looking at the map. "Are we going to walk all that way?"

"No time," said Marissa. "I think we can hire someone to give us a ride. You've got some money, right?"

"Not much," said Clara, pulling a few dollar bills from her pocket. "But I can turn it into more at the poker table."

They entered the second compartment of the press car, where the usual poker game was in full swing. Soon, Clara had a nice, large stack of money in front of her. Just a little bit more, Clara told herself, and they'd have enough for their journey.

"Five-card stud," announced Clement as he dealt two cards to each player, one facing down, the other facing up. Clara knew this game well. In five-card stud, there would only be one hidden card. The other four would be dealt faceup, one at a time.

Clement finished dealing the first two cards. Clara looked at hers. A four of diamonds was facing up. She lifted the corner of her hidden card. Five of diamonds. Nice start. She bet some of her money, and so did three other players.

Clement slapped another card faceup in front of Clara. The seven of diamonds. Her pulse quickened. She was close to a flush—

five cards of the same suit. She was also close to a straight—five numbers in a row. She bet some more. Gordon sighed and pushed his cards away. Phillips also folded.

But Burns matched her bet. He didn't have much in front of him—a three of hearts, and a six of spades. Plus whatever he was hiding in his facedown card. There was now a lot of money in the middle of the table.

The fourth card arrived, faceup.

An eight of diamonds for Clara.

Gordon whistled appreciatively. "Kid's riding a flush, Burnsy."

"Or a straight," said Clement.

Or both, thought Clara, remembering the five of diamonds hiding in front of her.

She tried not to look at the hidden five, keeping her face as calm as possible as she casually bet half of the money remaining in front of her.

Burns looked down at the cards in front of him, where a nine of clubs had just joined the three of hearts and the six of spades. He pursed his lips, looked up at Clara, and fixed her with a hard stare. The train whistle blew, and the clattering rhythm outside the window began to slow.

Clara tried not to show anything. She thought about all the money on the table, and how she and her sister would travel in style when it came time to leave the train. Maybe even get their own horses.

"Call," said Burns, interrupting Clara's daydream and matching the money Clara had put into the pot.

Clara tried to keep a straight face. She eagerly awaited the fifth and final card.

Clement licked his thumb and slid another card in front of Clara.

The ace of spades.

All of Clara's excitement turned to stone inside her stomach.

She had no flush. No straight. Just five random cards.

The train rattled hard as it entered a dark tunnel. The only light was the electric bulb swinging overhead, casting swerving shadows over the cards and the players.

"I bet whatever you have left," said Burns, who'd just added the queen of diamonds. Aside from the hidden card, his hand was a mess of nothing: a three, a six, a nine, and a queen—all different suits.

Clara looked at the small stack in front of her. It was a meager supply, but still more than they'd walked in with. She could fold now, and walk away with enough to at least get some kind of a ride from the station.

But Burns could be bluffing—pretending he had something to chase her away.

"Call," said Clara, pushing the rest of her money in.

Burns flipped over his hidden card.

The six of diamonds.

He put it next to his six of spades.

One pair.

Not a great hand.

Not even a good hand.

But a better hand than hers. She'd lost all the money.

Clara flipped over her useless five and slumped back in her seat. The train emerged from the tunnel and bright, harsh sunlight filled the compartment.

"Don't sweat it," said Burns as he swept all of her money into his pile. "Knowing when to quit is the hardest part."

Clara stood up without a word. She drifted into the baggage car, collapsed on a lumpy mail bag, and covered her face with her hands.

"No time for that," said Marissa. "We're going to be in Raymond in less than an hour."

"So?" asked Clara. "I'm not getting off this thing without money. We're broke!"

"Yeah, but we still gotta get over there and—"

"And what, fly to the tree?" said Clara. "You said yourself there's no time to walk." She shook her head and stomped against the trunk in front of her. "Burns was right. Knowing when to quit is the hardest part."

"But we can't quit now," said Marissa.

"Says who?" Clara asked. "Hey, crazy clubhouse thing," she shouted at the ceiling of the baggage car, "I want . . . to go"—she pulled her foot back and kicked hard against Ethel's trunk—"HOME!"

The trunk rolled over onto its side with a jingling noise.

The girls stared at the trunk.

"What was—"

Before Clara could finish her sentence, Marissa opened the trunk and started tossing its contents out onto the floor of the car.

Dresses, stockings, and shoes went flying as she dug farther and farther to the bottom, until the trunk was entirely empty.

Marissa shook her head in confusion. "But I thought I heard—"

"Yeah, I heard it too," said Clara. She started digging through the piles on the floor, while Marissa shoved the empty trunk out of the way. Again, the trunk made a jingling noise. The girls looked at each other, then attacked the trunk, pulling at the hinges and banging on the sides. Marissa found a loose corner on the satin lining. She pulled hard and the entire lining ripped away, revealing a single purple sock, bulging with coins, dollar bills, and a deck of cards.

"Clara," said Marissa, "we're back in business."

CHAPTER 20

FIRE IN THE HOLE!

"YOU sure Ethel won't mind?" asked Clara as Marissa counted up the glorious pile of cash on the wooden platform marked RAYMOND, CALIFORNIA.

"She specifically told me I could use her socks anytime," said Marissa.

The crowds were gone, and so was the train, just a faint whisper of smoke now, drifting into the rugged mountain sky. Marissa felt good. Confident. She took a deep breath of the cold, piney air. She was finally home in California.

Across the tracks was a tall, skinny man with bronze skin and long black hair checking the harness on a messy tan horse, connected to a wood-paneled wagon with flaking red paint and several rows of passenger benches shaded by a tattered black canopy.

"Hello . . ." said Marissa, walking up next to the man. "Do you know where the Steeple Giant is?"

"Yep," said the man.

"Can you take us to it?"

"Nope."

"Why not?" demanded Clara.

"Gone," said the man, giving a hard tug on one of the leather straps of the harness.

"No!" said Marissa, a little louder and sharper than she intended.

The man shrugged and went to the other side of the wagon to check the rest of the straps.

"Can we go see where it . . . was?" asked Marissa

The man shrugged again. He nodded his chin toward the back of the wagon. Marissa and Clara took the hint and climbed into one of the benches. The man took hold of the reins, then turned back toward Marissa with his hand out. Marissa took some money out of the purple sock and gave it to him. She wasn't sure if it was enough or way too much, but the man accepted it without expression, turned back to the front, and cracked the reins.

The wagon creaked forward. They spent the next several hours rattling up narrow and bumpy mountain tracks.

Clara grimly clung to the side of the bench, closing her eyes as the big wheels clunked over the stones of a dry riverbed. "I think I'm going to be sick," she moaned.

"Not on me, you're not," said Marissa, shifting to the far side.

"Where are we going?" asked Clara.

"Up," said the man.

The sun hung low through the sparse tree line as the wagon crossed into a wide valley, punctuated by stumps and fallen trees. The air grew colder. Single riders passed back and forth on horseback, as well as small groups of workmen crossing the road with axes and picks across their shoulders.

The girls caught sight of an old man who looked nothing like the workers, making his way through the woods about fifty yards from the road. His long, flowing beard made him look like a kind wizard. There was a flower tucked behind his ear.

More flatbed wagons passed in the opposite direction, pulled by teams of mules. Some wagons had small logs and boards, but others were taken up by single enormous logs held in place by chains, nearly filling the road with their swaying bulk.

"Gone," said the man from the front of the wagon, pointing at a particularly gigantic log passing by, its end exposed to show hundreds of rings.

"That's not big enough to be the Steeple Giant," Marissa responded with a touch of resentment. She wasn't giving up until she saw the stump with her own eyes. But she was becoming more and more nervous with every load of wood passing by in the other direction. Her one hope rested on the little pencil mark on the map: tomorrow's date. If the map was right, the tree was still there. One more day.

The surrounding landscape became harder to see in the gathering twilight. The horse labored to pull the wagon up the steep road. The man suddenly yanked on the reins and the wagon came to an abrupt stop.

"Why'd you stop?" asked Clara.

The man said nothing, and pointed at a hand-painted sign by the side of the road.

DANGER—BLAST ZONE—KEEP OUT

"Oh come on," said Marissa. "Just a little farther?"

He shook his head. He yanked the reins to the side, and the horse made a slow half circle, pointing the wagon back down the hill, and started trotting.

"Stop!" said Marissa.

"Dangerous," muttered the man, continuing to drive.

"Fine," said Marissa. She stood up and jumped off the moving wagon, tumbling into a ditch. The man gave an annoyed tug on the reins and the wagon stopped. He looked back at Clara expectantly. She sighed and climbed off the wagon, taking the bag with her.

"You OK?" Clara asked as the wagon rolled away down the hill.

"Yeah," Marissa said, pulling herself up out of the ditch.

"This is so depressing," said Clara.

"I know," said Marissa. "Look at this place."

"No, I mean it's depressing that I'm suddenly the one with common sense!" Clara said.

"You'll do something stupid soon enough."

"Hope so," said Clara. She looked around. "You sure this tree of yours is still out there?"

"No," said Marissa.

"So what now?"

"I don't know," said Marissa.

"OK," said Clara. "Let's wing it." She started walking away from the road.

"That's definitely not the right way," said Marissa, pulling out the map.

Clara turned around. "We wing it this way then!"

As evening turned into night, the girls left the road and headed for the top of the hill. When they reached the top, they saw a wide valley, bathed in yellow moonlight, covered in stumps. Row upon row of them. Like headstones.

It was quiet. No wind. No crickets. No birds.

A distant voice shouted, "FIRE IN THE HOLE!"

Suddenly the ground in front of the girls swelled like an ocean wave and burst into the evening sky. A shock wave of air smacked Marissa in the chest, knocking the breath out of her lungs. Only then did she hear the tremendous sound of the underground blast. Her feet tumbled over her head as her body flew backward down the hillside, hard over rocks and roots until she finally crashed to a bruising stop against the side of a boulder.

Marissa's mouth hung open as she gasped for air. Her ears rang. Her vision was purple. She was on her knees, hands on the ground. Someone was gripping her arm. She looked toward it, blinking over and over, trying to clear the purple clouds and willing her vision to return. Clara's face appeared through the haze, yelling at her, but Marissa couldn't hear a thing. Marissa made a feeble wave, then pitched forward onto the ground, enjoying the soft, cold dirt against her throbbing cheek as she closed her eyes and fell asleep.

CHAPTER 21

SARAH

THE ringing was endless. It just kept going and going and going.

There was a voice Marissa could barely hear, distant, hollow, scared, almost drowned out by the ringing, but not quite. Marissa tried opening her eyes but only managed a crack, through which she saw flames, bright orange and gold.

Marissa closed her eyes again and the voice grew louder, echoing through the endless ring and calling her name.

No, not calling her name. Calling her names.

"Hey, spazo!"

Marissa blinked her eyes feebly.

"Bozo!" Clara's voice called, louder and clearer. "Wake up wake up WAKE UP!"

Marissa opened her eyes again, wider this time, taking in the flames and the fireplace surrounding them. She was lying on her side, her head on a coarse pillow, inside a warm, log-sided room.

A cool hand was stroking her hair. The voice of an elderly woman was singing something comforting and soft.

The name-calling grew louder. "C'mon, freako," said Clara's voice, cracking desperately, "This isn't funny. Wake up!"

"Shut up," Marissa managed to whisper, "jerkface."

"She's back!" Clara exclaimed happily.

Marissa felt a surge of pain as her sister's arms wrapped her bruised ribs in a joyous hug.

"Oof," Marissa groaned.

"Want some salmon?" Clara asked with a mouth full of food. "Sarah cooked it up over the fire. You gotta try this."

"Sarah?" Marissa croaked in confusion. She tried to sit up, but the cool hand pressed her head back to the pillow.

"Rest," the elderly woman's voice said in a friendly command.

"Sarah found us after the dynamite went off," Clara explained. "I was yelling like a crazy person after you passed out, and she came up and brought us back to the cabin."

"The cabin," Marissa whispered, closing her eyes again. She remembered the hand-drawn map of the dam construction site. The little cabin marked *abandoned*. The stream running alongside it. And the tree on the other side.

Marissa's eyes flew open.

"The cabin!" Marissa repeated. She stood up and felt a pain in her stomach like a thousand needles poking her at the same time. The purple clouds swept back into her vision, and her legs turned to jelly. She lurched sideways and crashed into Clara, who held her up and ordered her to sit down.

Marissa brushed her off and stumbled to the door, reaching

its rope handle and pulling it open. The night air was cold and bracing. Marissa took a deep breath, and the purple clouds cleared from her vision. She limped forward into the night.

Ahead of her, the stream was right where the map said it would be. The moon danced against the flowing water, punctuated by rocks and logs up and down the creek bed. Marissa stepped into the stream, feeling the surprisingly strong and icy current against her ankles. She was awake now.

She took another step forward, feeling the weight of the water against her shoes. She took another step and gasped as the ground fell away beneath her, dropping her waist deep into the cold water.

She was swimming now, beating against the current, eyes fixed on the other side. She could make it, she knew. She heard Clara yelling behind her. She looked up at the ridgeline, seeing nothing but stars and the outlines of stumps and jagged land.

Farther across now, almost to the other side. Her feet found the ground and she waded out onto the steep and muddy embankment, soaking wet, eyes scanning desperately for the tree that she knew must be here if the map was right. Marissa scrambled up the patchy ground.

In the faint moonlight she saw only stumps and shadows playing out across the valley in front of her. Was the map wrong? Was the old giant already gone? She looked up at the sky, brilliantly lit with millions of stars. The stars began to melt as her eyes watered. She felt the weight of failure sweep over her.

She wiped her eyes and noticed something strange about the stars. They were everywhere—except right in front of her. In the

middle of the horizon, it was just black. She stared at the void until her eyes adjusted, and the blackness took shape. Reaching high into cloudless sky, blocking out the stars in its path, was a very large black outline.

In the shape of a very, very big tree.

Marissa gasped. She felt an electric surge of emotion as she stared at the massive trunk, wide as a school bus and black in the night, a looming tower straight up to the first branches of the crown, fifty feet off the ground.

"TREEEEEEEE!" Marissa shouted, arms raised in victory.

"What?" yelled Clara's distant voice.

"TREE! TREE! TREE!" yelled Marissa, stumbling across the open ground to the dark shadow. When she reached the tree, she grabbed hold of the wet bark and buried her nose in its vertical grooves, breathing in the rich, moist scent.

It felt alive, and real, and strong. A warm hum filled her muscles and seemed to lift her soul. The ringing in her ears went away. So did the pain. The excitement of discovery gave way to an overwhelming sense of calm, from her toes to her scalp.

Marissa walked along the base of the tree, climbing over giant roots and running her palms against a wall of wood that went on forever, curving inward and outward.

Suddenly a figure burst out of the darkness, seizing her roughly. Marissa cried out weakly as she fell to the ground, unable to move her arms.

"You found it!" Clara shouted in Marissa's ear as she hugged her tightly.

"Get off of me," Marissa grumbled.

"Why are you so wet?" asked Clara cheerfully as she released her sister and stood up.

"Why aren't you?" Marissa asked, painfully lifting herself to her feet. "How'd you get across the stream?"

"There's a little bridge that's like ten feet from where you crossed," said Clara. "Sarah showed me."

"Sarah showed you."

"So this is it, eh?" Clara said casually, poking the bark and looking up at the looming trunk. She took a running start and scrambled up the slope of one of the largest roots, reaching the tree trunk at a point that was over ten feet above the ground. She gripped the bark of the tree, jumped up, and tried to scramble upward. Instead she fell straight back to the ground.

"OK," Clara gasped, the wind knocked out of her. "Yeah, that's pain."

"Is everything well?" the elderly woman's voice called from around the trunk.

"Never better," Clara croaked.

A flickering lantern appeared around the far end of the tree and floated toward them. As the lantern drew closer, Marissa got her first real look at Sarah's face. It was warm and weathered, framed by long white hair hanging in two decorated braids.

As Marissa locked eyes with the woman, she felt a shock of recognition. She reached out for the tree to steady herself.

Sarah's friendly eyes narrowed into a questioning expression. "Is everything all right?"

"Yes," Marissa blurted, regaining some of her self-control. "I mean, yes, ma'am."

Sarah looked up at the tree and sighed. "This tree wasn't meant to be alone. They share roots with the others." She held out her lantern and the light danced across several nearby stumps. "They grow tall because they grow together." She looked at Marissa and Clara. "Come," she said, and walked down the hill.

As the girls followed the glowing lantern, Marissa grabbed her sister's arm and whispered, "Did you see her eyes?"

"Yeah, I know," Clara replied.

"They look just like Mom's," said Marissa.

Clara stopped. "I was going to say they look just like yours."

A gust of wind blew through the tree behind them.

As they entered the cabin, Marissa got her first good look around. There were beautiful shawls hanging from nails throughout the room. Near the fireplace was an unfinished blanket with an even staircase pattern, next to a basket filled with spools of yellow, red, and green yarn. Sarah took a log and added it to the fire, then handed Marissa a robe.

"You'll catch death in those wet clothes," Sarah said. Then she chuckled. "My mother used to say the same to me when I played in that stream."

"You grew up here?" Marissa asked as she changed into the robe and hung her clothes up to dry by the fire.

Sarah opened a basket and pulled a fresh salmon out. She placed the fish on a rack above the fire.

"I was raised nearby. This cabin wasn't here. Someone built it and left it after I was gone." She sighed. "I am a visitor now. A crazy old woman from Fresno, swimming upstream like these salmon."

"Are you here to save the tree?" asked Clara.

Sarah looked at her with a sad smile. "I am here to remember. I thought maybe someone should be with the tree in her final days." She nodded toward the door and said, "My grandmother taught me how to knit in the shade of that giant sequoia." Sarah picked up the unfinished blanket and gestured for the girls to sit. "You will help me," she said.

As the fire crackled, Sarah demonstrated the repetitive knitting motions as she added stitches to the colorful blanket. She handed the needles to Marissa. Marissa tried to imitate Sarah's technique, but her yarn kept slipping out of place. Eventually she got it going. Then she realized she'd gone too far in one direction, messing up the pattern. What had been an even staircase of repeating yellow and red and green now had a horizontal yellow line extending several inches in the wrong direction. She looked up to ask for help, but saw Sarah standing by the open door, looking out toward the tree.

"That tree must have a lot of memories for you," said Marissa.

"It holds the memories of countless generations, going back over a thousand years. Long before settlers came to build cabins like this," Sarah said, then indicated the direction of the construction site, "or dams like that." She shook her head. "This will always be their land, their tree." Sarah turned to spread out woven mats for the girls to sleep on. "But the tree also holds my memories. So my memory will hold the tree when it is gone."

"We're not going to let anything happen to that tree," said Clara, playing solitaire with Ethel's cards on the floor.

Sarah smiled. "I admire the fight in you."

Marissa attacked the blanket once more, trying to correct the mistake she'd made in the staircase pattern, but Sarah stopped her.

"That is part of the blanket now. You have added to its story."

Marissa bit her lip and continued on with her knitting, building off of the mistake to add more lines and patterns to the blanket.

Sarah nodded with approval. "It's in your blood. Don't ever forget."

They continued to knit long into the night, as the logs crackled in the fireplace and the wind rattled against the door, sweeping across the empty hills, where a single tree remained.

CHAPTER 22

HANDCUFFS

MARISSA woke up first and silently dressed in the cold, dark morning. She nearly slipped on the playing cards that Clara had left on the floor. Marissa picked up the cards and shoved them in her pocket so the same thing wouldn't happen to Sarah. Then she tiptoed outside.

At one end of the valley was the construction site, full of tools and machines, all empty and quiet. At the other end stood the giant red tree. Standing alone on the hillside, it looked far bigger than any living thing Marissa had ever seen, reaching up through the twilight of the predawn valley into the first rays of dawn, which gave a bright green glow to the thick crown of branches near the top. Extending up from the crown was a single thin trunk, a pyramid-shaped spike resembling the steeple of a grand cathedral.

The Steeple Giant.

Marissa walked up the ridge, dry sticks and dead branches crackling under her feet as she walked. As she got closer to the enormous trunk, she heard someone whistling. She looked up and saw a man scaling the sheer face of the tree without any tools or ropes. He looked like a spider crawling up a wall. At first Marissa assumed it was one of the workmen preparing to cut the tree down, but then she noticed his long, flowing beard. It was the old wizard-like man they'd seen walking along the road the night before.

"A miracle, isn't it?" he shouted down with a Scottish accent.

Marissa looked around to see if he was talking to someone else. But she was alone. "What?" she shouted back.

"They've found a way to 'improve' the beauty of the forest," the man shouted, resuming his upward climb, "by cutting down its groves, and burying all the thickets and wildflowers two hundred feet underwater."

"So, you're like a protester or something?" asked Marissa,

"God has cared for this tree through the centuries," the Scottish man declared, as if preaching in a church. "Saved it from drought, disease, and a thousand leveling storms."

He stopped climbing, and let go with one hand to point at the distant construction site where a carriage had arrived with a small group of men in suits. "But he cannot save it from fools."

Marissa looked over and saw men in suits had arrived at the construction site across the valley of stumps. Other men, dressed in work clothes, arrived on foot, carrying shovels and saws and other tools on their backs. A small crew gathered axes, spikes, and long, two-handled saws, and began walking up the valley toward the tree.

"Ah, the mighty tree hunters approach," shouted the Scottish man, continuing to scale the tree. "Funny thing about trees, they're rather easy prey. They don't know when to run."

Marissa felt her chest tighten. "Maybe you should get down from there," she shouted.

"Nonsense!" said the Scottish man, now bathed in the morning sunlight that was slowly creeping down the giant trunk. "It's quite glorious—I believe I can see Tokyo."

Marissa rubbed her forehead. "Listen, this is—"

"AWESOME!" yelled Clara, running up from the cabin with a big grin on her face. "You HAVE to show me how to get up there!"

"Clara, no!" said Marissa.

"Nothing to it!" the Scottish man shouted to Clara. "The channels in the bark form a lovely pathway up—easier for your small feet than mine!"

Clara took a run at the tree and tried to scale it, but slid back down.

Marissa heard the loggers approaching. She turned and awkwardly ran down toward them. The men all stopped moving and eyed her curiously. A large bearded man approached her. He looked like the statue of Paul Bunyan she'd seen when campaigning with her mom in Minnesota.

"Are you lost, little girl?" he asked.

"No, I'm not," said Marissa. "I'm here to ask you . . ." Her throat went dry. All the little speeches she'd planned were stuck in her brain. She felt her courage fading.

She looked down and saw a long, snaking root running along the ground. She followed it with her eyes and saw that it extended all the way back to the Steeple Giant. Her eyes followed it forward and saw that it intertwined with the roots of several of the leveled stumps. Family.

She lifted her head and said, "Listen, you can't cut that tree down. It's all that's left of this family."

"Miss," the bearded man said kindly but firmly, "we're hired to do a job, and we're going to do it."

"Yeah, but . . ."

Think, Marissa told herself, change the math. All you need is time. Just more time. She felt the deck of cards in her pocket.

"Who wants to play poker?" asked Marissa.

"ME!" said one of the loggers.

"Me too!" said another, dropping a coil of rope and sitting down eagerly.

"No!" said the bearded man. "You all know the rules."

The loggers all nodded sheepishly. The seated man stood up, picked up his rope, and started heading toward the tree. The others reluctantly followed.

"Why not?" asked Marissa, anxious to stall the workers as long as possible. "Just for a few hands?"

"They're not allowed to play poker," said the bearded man. "They fight too much."

"OK," said Marissa, "how about something else? Kings in the Corner? War?"

"We fight over those too," said the man with the rope.

"'Cause some people cheat," said a tall man carrying a short ladder.

"I do not!" shouted the man with the rope.

"I asked you did you have any fives," the other man said, tossing his ladder to the ground angrily, "and you had the five of hearts, but you said go fish anyways. YOU SAID GO FISH!"

The first man tossed his rope on a stump, fists clenched, eyes burning. "Why, you lying, no-good . . ."

"Trouble seems to follow you wherever you go," said a low, flat voice behind Marissa.

Marissa looked over her shoulder and found herself staring up at the black mustache and blank round spectacles of Mr. Loeb. He grabbed her by the arm.

"Let GO of me!" shouted Marissa.

"So you can sabotage me once more?" asked Mr. Loeb coldly. "I think not."

Marissa tried to speak, but no words came out. Mr. Loeb marched Marissa across the valley down to the hillside where the men in suits were gathered. He pushed her up a set of rickety wooden stairs that led to a large platform holding several offices and tents clustered together in a makeshift headquarters. Looking down, Marissa realized the entire platform was really one giant stump. She stared down at the lines in the wood. There were hundreds.

"YOU!" shouted a voice.

Marissa looked up to see Wendell marching toward her, eyes wide, clutching a wilted carnation in his lapel to keep it in place in the rising wind.

"Do you have any idea how much it cost me to find another train out of that silly wilderness?" he screeched.

"Arnold," Mr. Loeb said in a calming voice.

"We had no food!" shouted Wendell. "No lobster, no steak—no cigars! Not one cigar on that miserable little caboose!"

"That's all behind us now," said Mr. Loeb.

"Not even a cookie!"

"Arnold," said Mr. Loeb.

"Get her off my property!" Wendell shouted.

"This is not your property, it is state land," Mr. Loeb corrected him.

"Details!" Wendell shouted.

A sharp gust of wind tore through the valley and ripped the carnation away. Wendell chased after it and fell off the side of the stump.

A brief smile twitched across Mr. Loeb's face. His expression returned to stone.

"Jeffrey!" Mr. Loeb called.

The red-haired Jeffrey came running up. Apparently he'd caught up after his adventure with the bull. And he'd gotten a brand-new bowler hat. He nodded and pulled Marissa's hands behind her.

"Hey!" said Marissa. "What are you—"

"Shh," said the Jeffrey.

Marissa felt cold iron close around her right wrist.

"No!" said Marissa, her heart racing. She tried to yank her hand away and felt a sharp pain where the metal dug into her skin.

"Stop," the Jeffrey said quietly.

"Never!" said Marissa.

She felt cold iron close around her left wrist as well. She heard a click, then the turn of a key. She yanked against the metal but her hands stayed trapped behind her. She was handcuffed.

Her lower lip quivered. She felt the world collapsing around her. She was under arrest.

"What are you going to do about her?" demanded Wendell, climbing back onto the stump, his expensive suit torn and muddy.

"I'm going to charge her, Arnold," said Mr. Loeb.

"With what?" demanded Marissa.

"What's your preference?" Mr. Loeb asked lightly. "Trespassing? Damage to railroad property?" He reached into his briefcase and pulled out a newspaper. "Or maybe you'd prefer theft of government property!" he said, showing anger for the first time as he snapped open the newspaper.

It was the evening edition of the *San Francisco Call*.

And there, below the fold but still on the front, was a pen-and-ink drawing of a crying girl clinging to a tree, and the headline "Schoolchildren Roiled by Industry Baron's Scheme, Bank Ponders Retreat." Gordon had snagged the front page after all.

"Interesting story, this," said Mr. Loeb. "There are several details in here that could only have come from my personal files."

"Let me go!" said Marissa.

"I intend to prosecute," Mr. Loeb said through clenched teeth, "to the fullest extent—"

A loud crack echoed across the valley.

One of the loggers stood by the giant tree, pulling his ax from its side. Marissa felt a sharp pain in her gut. Another crack echoed as a second man swung his ax into another part of the tree a few feet away from the first. A third man joined them, and a fourth, driving their blades into different sections of the ancient living wood.

Mr. Loeb walked away to speak with one of the other men in suits. Marissa struggled against the handcuffs, but the Jeffrey held her back.

"Those are made for adult criminals," the Jeffrey said quietly. "You can't just break out of them."

Another cracking noise, then another and another. Bright red marks were appearing where the outer bark had been penetrated along the base of the Steeple Giant.

Marissa looked around for her sister but couldn't see her anywhere. "Clara!" she yelled.

"Quiet, kid," said Wendell.

"No," said Marissa. "I won't."

"I hate children," Wendell grumbled.

The cracking sounds multiplied. The entire work crew was now hacking at different points in the tree.

"Mr. Wendell, please," Marissa said, her voice breaking.

"We must build this nation's future!" Wendell declared.

"By destroying its past?" asked Marissa.

"You have to crack eggs to make breakfast," said Wendell.

"What?"

"Someday you'll understand."

"No," said Marissa, "I won't. Listen, that tree right there means a lot to me. I can't explain it, it just . . . calls me, all right?"

"Not my problem," said Wendell.

"Haven't you ever felt a connection to something, so powerful you just can't put it into words?" asked Marissa.

Wendell turned to Marissa, eyes suddenly wide and emotional. "Yes," he said softly, "yes, there was something. A long time ago."

Marissa felt a spark of hope in her chest. "What was it?"

"The first dollar I ever made," Wendell said in a faraway voice, looking up at the sky.

"Oh," said Marissa, feeling the hope extinguish. "Well, I mean, wasn't there anything else that called you like that?"

"Yes," Wendell said, turning back to her, voice trembling with sincere emotion, "every dollar I've ever made since."

Mr. Loeb returned and said, "We finally appear to be back on schedule, Mr. Wendell, barring any unexpected— oh turtle soup."

Marissa followed Mr. Loeb's gaze as he stared at the tree with a tight frown. Then she saw the same thing he did: an old man with a long beard, high above the loggers, was scaling the face of the tree. And right alongside him, confidently working her way up the deep grooves of the tree without a rope or a net, was a nine-year-old girl.

CHAPTER 23

THE BRANCH

"CLARA!" Marissa yelled.

"Halt operations!" Mr. Loeb yelled.

"Absolutely not!" said Wendell.

"Have you lost your senses?" asked Mr. Loeb. "We must pause to extract the trespassers."

"Nix!" said Wendell.

As the two men argued, the chopping continued to echo across the valley.

"Stop!" Marissa cried desperately. She yanked hard against the handcuffs.

"I already told you, kid," said the Jeffrey, "those are adult handcuffs. Too strong to break."

"Let me GO!" said Marissa.

"You remember that bull ride back in Dakota?" the Jeffrey quietly asked. "Most thrilling eight seconds of my life. But that bull would have killed me for sure if you hadn't stepped in."

"So this is how you repay me?" growled Marissa. "Sticking me in handcuffs?"

"Yes," said the Jeffrey, then added, "Adult handcuffs."

Marissa yanked against the iron restraints once more, and thought about what he'd just said. Adult handcuffs. She relaxed her hands and pointed them to the ground. And the cuffs, several sizes too big, fell right off.

"Oops," said the Jeffrey.

Marissa sprinted toward the Steeple Giant, leaping over ditches and scrambling over rocks.

"STOP!" she yelled. "STOP!"

The bearded foreman turned at her voice and waved her off.

"Hey!" he yelled at Marissa. "It's not safe here!"

"That's my sister up there!" Marissa yelled back, finger in the air.

The foreman's eyes traveled up the tree. He saw nothing. Marissa grabbed him by the arm and led him around to the other side. Way up into the mist, he saw Clara.

The foreman put his big hand to his forehead. He turned and shouted, "STAND DOWN!"

The loggers stopped chopping. The valley fell silent.

Then another voice howled up from the construction site.

"NOOOOO!" shouted Wendell, huffing and puffing up the hill to the tree in his muddy suit, gripping the damaged carnation in his hand. "Don't you dare stop working!"

Forty feet in the air, Clara was clinging to the side of the tree, but Wendell's voice still carried loud enough to make her glance down. She immediately regretted it. She saw the loggers leaning on their axes and staring up at her. The ground seemed to stretch out below her.

Clara closed her eyes and looked up, the first real branch still ten feet above her. Her palms were sweating. She dug her feet into the grooves of the tree as a gust of wind drove a chill through her.

"Out of my way!" Wendell's voice shrieked below.

This was followed by a loud thud. Clara looked down and saw Wendell, tiny in the far distance below, wielding an ax, taking clumsy chops at the tree.

"You'll hurt yourself!" one of the loggers shouted.

"This work will proceed!" yelled Wendell.

Clara watched as he tried and failed, again and again, to drive the head of an ax into the wood. The ground began to swim again. Clara's guts churned. She swallowed hard. Her arms were shaking and her fingers ached at the knuckles, getting slimy at the tips. She looked up at the Scottish man, who was sitting ten feet above her on the first branch, his long beard sailing in the wind.

"Keep going!" he urged. "The view is better up here."

Clara released her right-hand grip and immediately clenched back to the safety of the soft bark.

"Move!" the old man urged.

"I can't!" said Clara, panic beginning to seep in.

"Malarkey," said the man. "Up you go."

Another crack echoed from below. Clara glanced down and felt her vision extend into a yawning tunnel, with Wendell at the end, awkwardly swinging his ax against the side of the tree, then reeling back in pain as the loggers watched with amusement.

Clara squeezed her eyes shut and tried to slow her breathing. Another crack sounded from below, and in spite of herself, Clara let out a light whimper.

"Aw, don't mind him," the Scottish man said, "his technique is terrible."

The Scottish man stood up on the wide branch and assumed a low stance.

"Now, the proper way to bury an ax is to let your legs do all the work," he said, demonstrating wide, powerful swings into the trunk. "That'll bring her down in a hurry."

"You're not helping," said Clara, willing herself to let go with the left hand.

"It'll take that fool weeks to bring this down with such incompetent technique," the Scottish man said with disdain.

Clara managed to creep up about six inches.

"Ach, child, you've made it up this far," said the Scottish man, squatting on the branch and looking down, his beard curled hard to the left in the mountain wind. "What's another ten feet?"

"It's getting harder," Clara cried.

"Of course it's getting harder!" he said. "There's less bark near the crown. That last stretch is like scaling a greased pole."

"Can you stop talking, please?" grunted Clara.

The Scottish man grinned and sat against the trunk, whistling.

With effort, Clara yanked her right foot out of a tight channel in the bark and raised it higher, her toe slipping on the wet, smooth surface until finally finding a slight toehold. She felt her limbs cramping. With a determined burst, she straightened her body and climbed higher.

"Don't rest!" the Scottish man shouted. "Keep moving!"

Easy for you to say, Clara thought. Her breathing quickened. And the wind picked up. The entire tree creaked and moaned. Clara could feel it as much as hear it. A low rumble rolled in from the mountains.

"Storm coming!" the Scottish man yelled cheerfully.

A hard gust pressed Clara into the trunk. She clung tightly to the soft wood, wishing she were already on the branch. Or back on the ground. Or back home in her bed. Anywhere but here. Anywhere. She buried her face in the channels of the tree, breathing hard and quick in short, panicking gasps.

The wet wooden smell filled her lungs. And the energy of the tree began to fill her body. She reached a hand up and hoisted herself further. Another foot higher. She released her left hand and clung higher. Followed by her right. Then she moved her feet.

The wind died down, leaving a cloud of mist surrounding Clara. She couldn't see up anymore. She couldn't see down. Everything was gray. She heard her sister's voice below, shouting and arguing with Wendell. Clara looked to her left and her right and found nothing. She was in the cloud. She was part of the cloud. The Scottish man was shouting words of encouragement, but he sounded a thousand miles away. Clara heard only the tree now. Only the creaks, and the groans, and the whispers through the branches.

Four feet now. Three. The huge branch was above her now.

Clara clung to the tree once more. She buried her face in its wood. She breathed in its piney smell, and a strange feeling of calm came over her. She felt like the tree was holding her as much as she was holding it. Clara scrambled up the last three feet, then pulled herself up and around the big branch and collapsed on top.

Finally able to rest, Clara shivered with nervous energy and exhaustion. She looked out over the work site. In every direction were stumps and mud. Smoke was rising from the chimney of Sarah's cabin. On the mountain road beyond, several wagons were winding their way into the construction site, crowded with passengers.

On the ground, Marissa recognized the lead wagon. And she recognized the driver. He was the same man who had driven them up from the station. Marissa ran down to meet the wagon as its passengers climbed off. They looked like they were dressed for a picnic. They pointed in amazement at the Steeple Giant.

"Who are all these people?" Marissa asked.

The driver waved a copy of the *San Francisco Call*. The other wagons added over a dozen more people, including a family with two girls and a boy, who all stared openmouthed at the giant tree.

"Come on!" Marissa yelled to the people. "Follow me!"

The people looked at Marissa blankly, then went back to admiring the tree from a distance. Wendell's ax continued to thud against its trunk. Several people began to set out picnic blankets.

"Don't you guys want to stop them?" asked Marissa.

"Such a shame," said a man lying on a blanket, propped up on his elbow and smoking a pipe.

"At least we were able to see it," said a woman in a purple hat, "before it had to go."

Marissa looked around desperately. Change the math, she thought. Change the math. Change the math. Then her eye landed on the three children. She walked up to them. She poked the tallest girl and said, "Tag! You're it!" She ran up the hill toward the tree, with three children chasing her.

"Oh for heaven's sake!" Wendell cried when he saw Marissa arrive with the three children. "They're multiplying!" He took another swing at the tree.

"Stop it!" yelled the taller girl.

"Yeah!" yelled the other girl, who had a blue ribbon in her hair.

"Boo!" yelled the boy.

Several of the loggers laughed and joined in. "Boo!" they yelled.

"I will not be mocked!" screamed Wendell.

"Too late!" yelled a lumberjack.

"Arnold," Mr. Loeb said as he climbed up the hill, "there is no need to rush things."

"No need?" Wendell screeched. He pointed at the road where the red wagon had returned with another six passengers. "We're being invaded by tourists! The more people start visiting, the more people who'll start whining. And God forbid they start voting. Then we lose finance and time and support and . . . and . . . shall we surrender the world to children?!?"

With that, he swung back his ax for a mighty chop but lost his grip. The ax flew through the air, rotating wildly as it headed straight for Mr. Loeb, who ducked just in time to avoid losing his head.

"My word, sir!" Mr. Loeb shouted. "Get ahold of yourself!"

"I will not!" yelled Wendell. He marched over to the neat stack of tools to pick up another ax. One of the lumberjacks stood up, got in his way, and shook his head. Wendell backed up, pointed his finger at the man, then ran away. Everybody cheered.

As Wendell disappeared down the hillside, the wind picked up and the sky grew darker. Mr. Loeb walked over to the base of the tree, shaded his eyes, and stared up into the branches. "This is not safe," he said.

"No kidding," said Marissa.

The tree creaked, groaned, and whispered. With no other trees around it to shield its branches, the Steeple Giant took the full brunt of the wind, visibly bending near the top.

"You have to order her to get down," Mr. Loeb said.

"Order her?" Marissa asked. "You don't know much about siblings, do you?"

"Very well," Mr. Loeb said, sounding nervous. "Ask her." Then he added, "Please."

Another gust cut through, carrying with it a purple hat. A stack of tools toppled over, and a page from the *San Francisco Call* went spiraling up and away.

Marissa cupped her hands to her mouth and yelled, "Clara! I think you've made your point now! Come on down!"

At that point, Clara sincerely wished she could follow her sister's advice. But the wind was twice as strong in the crown of the tree as it was at the base. She clung to her wide branch with both arms and both legs, feeling it bounce and shudder with every gust. Through the thick branches above her she saw the steeple-shaped spire of the tree whipping back and forth in a mad frenzy. Hard drops of rain started to join the cold mist. The Scottish man leaned against the tree trunk and lit a pipe.

"Ever weathered a storm in the topmast of a ship?" he asked.

"No," Clara groaned, feeling her salmon dinner churning in her stomach with every sway of the ancient tree.

"Neither have I," he said. Then he brightened. "I have spent a storm in a tree, though."

"How was that?" asked Clara.

"Terrifying," he said with a grin.

Clara looked down and saw raindrops speeding away from her onto the people below. Marissa was yelling something she could barely hear and waving for her to come down. Beside Marissa was Mr. Loeb, staring straight up into the rain. In the distant road beyond, a group of riders approached.

The wind built steadily, punctuated by occasional gusts of wind so fierce that they threatened to knock Clara off her perch. Charcoal-colored clouds advanced over the valley, shedding diagonal trails of rain across the shadowed fields below. The Scottish man started to sing.

Clara turned her head and rested her cheek against the soft bark of her branch. The wind tore at her hair and ears. The massive trunk creaked and swayed. Clara's branch bounced up and down. She felt a wave of sickness pass through her from head to toe and back. Far below, the lumberjacks carried their tools to shelter down the hill. Mr. Loeb left as well, heading for the office tents.

Clara looked down and saw two people at the tree. On one side was Marissa, standing alone, getting pelted by the gathering storm. On the other side of the massive tree was Wendell, with a canvas bundle in his arms. As Clara watched from fifty feet above, Wendell unwrapped the bundle and took red sticks out, placing them in the corners and cracks of the tree.

"Is that dynamite?" Clara gasped.

"It would appear so," the Scottish man said thoughtfully, squatting and looking down. "That would certainly accelerate the timeline." He stood up and tried to relight his wet pipe.

Clara tried to yell for her sister, but the words wouldn't squeak out of her mouth. The wind was now swirling around the tree, gusting from both directions at once.

"You there," the old man yelled down to Wendell, "do you realize how much good lumber you'll waste if you blast us into toothpicks?"

"Stay out of this!" Wendell shouted up as he used a spool of black fuse wire to connect the red sticks.

"I'm afraid we're quite in this!" the Scottish man shouted back cheerfully.

At the sound of Wendell's voice, Marissa scrambled around the tree, slipping and tripping over giant roots. She saw the dynamite and screamed. One of the lumberjacks ran over and yelled, "Fire in the hole!"

At the bottom of the hill, Mr. Loeb stepped out of his tent and lifted his binoculars. "Arnold, you clown!" he yelled.

Lightning streaked across the sky, and a crack of thunder rolled against the hills. Clara clung tighter than ever to her branch, tasting acid. Her stomach churned. She squeezed her eyes shut. The branch sank low and bounced high, moving up and down in the shifting wind.

She opened her eyes again to see Wendell standing directly beneath her, attempting to unspool the fuse wire. The branch shook harder. The tree swayed further. The gaping emptiness below Clara seemed to stretch to infinity, and a putrid taste trickled into her mouth as a shiver jolted her spine. Then, all at once, the contents of her stomach exploded through her mouth as she vomited over the branch, down into the air below.

Wendell continued his clumsy efforts, ignoring the shouting voices and the howling wind. The rain on his neck only urged him on. The drops became a flood. Stomach fluid and vomit and fresh salmon chunks cascaded over him. The loggers groaned and laughed and howled. He dropped the spool and looked up to see what had hit him. The last drop fell in his eye.

CHAPTER 24

THE DRAWING BOARD

FIFTY feet above the puke-soaked businessman, Clara wiped her mouth and squeezed her eyes shut, more embarrassed than she'd ever been in her entire life. But her stomach felt better.

The Scottish man looked down at the mess below. "That's one way to delay a project," he said with a smile. "More satisfying than a petition."

Clara groaned and rested her check against the rough bark, staring off to the south, watching as three horseback riders approached from the road. As they got closer, Clara saw something that made her sit up. She shielded her eyes to make sure what she was seeing was real. Then she started to laugh.

"Something you'd like to share?" asked the Scottish man.

Clara pointed. The Scottish man strained his eyes toward the riders. "Well then," he said, nodding in recognition, "this may change things."

On the ground below, Mr. Loeb dropped his binoculars and ran to the tree, looking ready to punch Wendell. But the smell and the mess covering Wendell made Mr. Loeb take a sharp step back.

One of the men from the office tents came running up the hill with the binoculars. "Sir?" he said.

"I don't need those anymore," said Mr. Loeb, waving off the binoculars. "Tell Jeffrey to arrest Mr. Wendell for extreme idiocy."

"Yes, sir," said the man, holding out the binoculars, "but in the meantime I really think you ought to take a look at those riders."

Mr. Loeb grabbed the binoculars. He pointed them toward the riders. And his face fell. He lowered the binoculars and handed them back. He looked at his feet, cleared his throat, and addressed Marissa politely. "I suppose you and I should go greet the president."

Marissa looked at the riders. To the left was an elderly man. To the right was a young woman. And in the center,

leading the charge in a cavalry hat, was a rider with a red bushy mustache, and a grin that could be spotted from miles away.

When Roosevelt arrived at the tree, he dismounted and stared upward, eyes filled with wonder. He walked up to the tree, examining the bark and the roots.

"Alice, you were right," Roosevelt said. "This is a remarkable specimen of *Sequoiadendron giganteum*—well worth the morning ride."

Alice dismounted and walked over to Marissa. "I figured this is where you'd run off to."

"Thanks for getting him out here," Marissa whispered back.

"My father can always be talked into a horseback ride," said Alice.

Senator Mattoon awkwardly dismounted from the third horse, stretching and wincing in pain. He frowned in surprise at the crowd of picnickers, many of whom were now approaching the tree with excitement as they recognized the president.

Roosevelt walked slowly around the tree. He rested his hand on the side of a large root and closed his eyes.

"It's a church," he said, looking up into the branches with reverence. "A holy cathedral surpassing any of man's creations."

"Sir," said Mr. Loeb, "if I may—"

"You may not," said Roosevelt, then added, "Nice of you to join us, Loeb."

Roosevelt continued pacing around the tree, grinning wildly. He settled in between two large roots and sank to a seated position, letting his head drift back against the trunk and looking straight up into the branches.

He frowned and asked, "Are there people in this tree?"

"You've got my vote!" the Scottish man yelled from the sky.

"Dare greatly!" yelled Clara.

Roosevelt gave a small wave. Then he jumped up and said, "I wish to join them up there."

"Sir, I would not advise that," said Mr. Loeb.

"You don't think I could manage the climb?" Roosevelt said, sticking his chin out like a little boy.

"The tree is wired with explosives," said Mr. Loeb.

The president's smile disappeared. He walked farther along the base and came to the first of the red sticks wedged in a crevice of the tree. He stared at it. He shook his head.

"Who is responsible for this?" Roosevelt asked quietly.

No one answered at first. Then Wendell came running over. He was still covered in Clara's dinner, but that didn't stop him from putting on a winning smile and extending his hand to the president.

"My idea, sir," he said. "The progress of the nation depends on—"

"With a child in the branches?" Roosevelt snarled, ignoring the offered handshake and taking an aggressive step toward the businessman.

Wendell took a step back, raising his hands defensively. "I was just trying to encourage her to climb back down."

"And then, as soon as she set foot on the ground, you were going to detonate this shrine," said Roosevelt.

"Well, sir," Wendell said, "even shrines have to give way to progress. To build the transcontinental railroad, they had to move a few churches."

"They didn't shoot cannonballs through the stained-glass windows!" Roosevelt cried. He shook his head. "Shocks the very conscience."

Roosevelt yanked out the first stick of dynamite and casually stuck it under his arm. "Shocks the very conscience," he repeated as he followed the fuse to the next stick and pulled that one out as well.

"Sir," said Mr. Loeb, "maybe you shouldn't—"

"Indeed I shouldn't," said Roosevelt. He collected the remaining dynamite sticks and tossed the loose bundle to Mr. Loeb, who caught it with a whimper.

"Firecrackers in the hands of schoolboys," Roosevelt growled in disgust. "An unworthy end for such a magnificent specimen."

Roosevelt sniffed the air. He turned toward Wendell with distaste.

"Mr. Wendell," the president said, "are you familiar with the direct link between a man's health and his attentiveness to personal hygiene?"

Wendell's smile froze. "What was that, Mr. President?"

"He said you need a good soakin'," said one of the loggers.

Roosevelt turned to the logger and raised a curious eyebrow. "Do I know you?"

The man stood, saluted, and said, "First Volunteer Cavalry, sir."

"Another Rough Rider?" Marissa asked quietly.

"They're *everywhere*," Alice replied.

Roosevelt grinned and wrapped his arm around the man. "Now, here is a fellow who knows that gunpowder is for combat, not for pruning the shrubberies."

"That's true, Mr. President," the man said. "We were planning on just cutting her down with wedges and—"

"Where would you set the wedges?" asked Roosevelt with eager curiosity. He listened like a ten-year-old at the zoo.

"We cut notches into the trunk at a narrow point above the roots, see?" the lumberjack said. "Then we fix wedges into the trunk to make a platform, and stand on the platform to use two-man saws on the trunk."

"Marvelous, marvelous," said the president. "I never had the opportunity to work a two-man felling saw myself—trees don't grow this thick in Dakota."

"If you like, you can try it now," said the Rough Rider. "I'll get on the other end with you."

The president grinned even wider. "I'd love to—*love* to. But I believe we're going to leave this tree standing."

Marissa's heart leapt. Did she hear that right?

"Uuuuuum, Mr. President?" said Wendell, now being restrained by the red-haired Jeffrey. "Lovely she is, I agree, but the progress of a nation demands that—"

"Mr. Wendell, you are to be congratulated," said Roosevelt.

"I am?" Wendell responded enthusiastically.

"Indeed, sir!" said Roosevelt. "On this journey, I've had the benefit of many wise counselors." He turned and nodded at Alice. He tipped his hat to Marissa. He bowed respectfully to Mr. Loeb.

"I've discussed the matter with political and financial leaders." He looked at the old senator and Rigby Jr.

"And I've talked"—and he turned dramatically to the gathering tourists who now stood close by—"with the FOLKS!" And the people cheered.

Roosevelt was in his element, warming up with the energy of the crowd. "But with all due respect to the people, to the leaders, to my daughter, and"—he turned to Marissa, and looked up in the tree at Clara—"to brave and mysterious youngsters willing to spend themselves in the arena for a worthy cause, NO ONE"—he turned and put a finger in the face of Wendell—"NO ONE has made a better argument for the permanent preservation of this NATIONAL TREASURE than YOU DID, with your BLATANT ACT OF WAR, against a PLANT!"

"Thank you?" said Wendell.

The Jeffrey led him away.

With his arm still around the Rough Rider, Roosevelt addressed the lumberjacks.

"You men do fine work," the president said. "I do not ask that lumbering be stopped at all—quite the contrary. But I do hope for the preservation of the giant trees like this one, simply because it would be a shame to our civilization to let them disappear. They are the only ones of their kind in the world. Monuments in themselves."

Then he looked up and yelled, "And we do not climb monuments!"

"Sorry," Clara's voice called down.

"Someone get a rope, please," said Roosevelt.

Soon Clara was being lowered down with a rope tied around her waist. As soon as she hit the ground, she ran to Marissa and gave her a hug.

"Don't ever let me do that again," Clara said.

The rope went back up and the Scottish man gleefully rappelled down. When he reached the ground, Roosevelt was there to greet him.

"I must know, sir," said Roosevelt, grabbing the Scottish man's arm, "is there a self-sustaining ecosystem in the crown?"

"I believe so, Mr. President!" answered the Scottish man cheerfully. "Fresh soil and plants growing all by themselves!"

"Remarkable," smiled Roosevelt, throwing his arm around the man. "Any evidence of nesting birds? You *must* give me details of all you saw up there!"

From the crowd, a man in a checkered suit ran forward. "Mr. President!" he called. "You must join us at the Wanona Hotel for a grand banquet in your honor!"

"He'd rather climb a tree," said Alice to Marissa under her breath.

"Oh, thank you, but we won't be needing a meal this evening," said Roosevelt.

"But sir!" said the man in the suit. "We'll have lobster!"

Clara felt sick at the thought of more seafood. "Don't you have something normal, like chicken wings?" she said.

"We can have chicken wings!" the manager said.

"*Aaaaand* drumsticks?" Roosevelt asked.

"And drumsticks," the man answered.

"In that case, count on me to be there."

Yes, Clara thought, because her appetite was suddenly back.

"Loeb!" said Senator Mattoon as he charged through the gathering rain over to Mr. Loeb, waving his hands. "You've got to do something!"

"The president has spoken," said Mr. Loeb. "I don't create policy, I enforce it."

"But what about our project?" cried Senator Mattoon. "Our big, beautiful project!" he whined, stomping a mud puddle in his expensive shoes.

"I believe we must return to the drawing board," said Mr. Loeb, "and find a way to preserve the tree."

"But I HATE the drawing board!" Senator Mattoon howled, like a five-year-old who wants a toy but doesn't get it.

"Calm down!" called the girl with the blue ribbon in her hair.

"You can't tell me what to do!" shouted Senator Mattoon.

"How about me?" said the girl's father. "I vote in this state. Doesn't that mean I get to tell you what to do?"

Senator Mattoon held up his hands and said, "Well, of course, we can have an adult conversation about—"

"I think we've had enough adult conversations," said a woman in a yellow dress, holding up an umbrella against the rain. "Maybe we should listen to the kids for once."

"Save the tree!" yelled the boy.

"Save the tree!" yelled the tall girl.

"Save the tree!" yelled the adults.

"ALL RIGHT!" Senator Mattoon yelled, then added, "I'll take it under advisement." And he ran off through the streams of mud now coursing down the barren slope, with the crowd of children and adults following close behind.

"Feel that?" asked Alice.

"The rain?" asked Marissa.

"No," said Alice. "The math is changing."

Marissa allowed herself a small smile.

"Miss Roosevelt," said a low, flat voice right behind them. Marissa jumped in surprise.

"Mr. Loeb!" said Alice with exaggerated delight, turning and spilling water from her umbrella onto Mr. Loeb's shoes. "Lovely to see you once more!"

"Indeed," said Mr. Loeb, his mustache drooping in the rain. "I believe I must make an apology."

"You don't have to—" said Marissa.

"I wasn't speaking to you," he said. "In fact, I should have you arrested. Again."

"Except," said Alice, "you know the president won't stand for that."

"Yes," said Mr. Loeb, "of course. This girl will remain free."

"Gee, thanks," said Marissa.

"Don't push it," muttered Alice.

Mr. Loeb turned to Clara and said, "I do, however, owe an apology to *this* young lady. Please let me say that I am very sorry that . . . you were . . ."

"Almost killed by your dumb friend?" offered Clara.

"Quite," said Mr. Loeb.

"That's OK," said Clara. "Sorry I broke your train and left you to be eaten by wolves."

"As touching as all this is," said Alice, scanning the quickly darkening horizon, "has anyone seen my father lately?"

"THERE!" shouted Clara, pointing at two riders galloping away, straight into the approaching storm. One was President Roosevelt, on his brown-and-white horse. The other, on Alice's gray horse, was the Scottish man.

Alice and Mr. Loeb both threw their hands up in frustration.

"Unbelievable," said Mr. Loeb.

"You turn your back for a moment," said Alice.

"And he's gotten into more mischief!" said Mr. Loeb.

A crash sounded from the work site at the bottom of the hill. Several tents were on the ground. Office papers blew across the valley. Mr. Loeb and Alice ran toward the chaos.

Marissa and Clara headed for the cabin as the rain and wind intensified.

"Sarah!" yelled Clara as she threw open the door. "We saved the tree!"

But the cabin was dark and empty. Sarah was gone, and so were all of her things—except one. In the center of the clean-swept floor was the blanket they had worked on the night before, now completed. A small note sat on top. *For your journey.*

"She's gone?" asked Clara incredulously.

Marissa ran outside and looked up at the road, now clogged with the wagons and carriages of tourists and workers and executives all jumbled up in a hopeless traffic jam trying to escape the rising storm. She couldn't see Sarah anywhere.

Marisssa walked up the hill, trying to get a better view. She wrapped the blanket around her shoulders as the temperature dropped. A horizontal streak of lightning shot across the sky, followed by a clap of thunder that echoed through the mountains. The Steeple Giant's trunk groaned and creaked. Black clouds moved swiftly over the top of the tree. Dry, electric air swirled upward along the ground, tossing sticks and dust into the sky.

"Marissa," said Clara, running over with a funny smile, "your hair . . ."

"So is yours," said Marissa, reaching out to touch the static strands of her sister's hair that were floating up toward the sky.

Then lightning struck the Steeple Giant.

CHAPTER 25

MY TREE

JUST a tiny strip of light.

A quiet blink, connecting the clouds to the tree.

Then the air ripped apart with a horrific bang as all three hundred feet of the Steeple Giant lit up. Bark exploded from the trunk. Marissa fell on top of Clara and felt hot embers striking the blanket that was still wrapped around her shoulders.

Everything faded to a quiet, steady hum. Marissa rolled off of Clara. Her cheeks were wet and her skin was hot. A disgusting electric smell filled the air.

But the tree was still standing.

Smoking and black, chunks of bark missing up and down the trunk. But still there.

A tiny orange light appeared at the top of the tree.

"No," Marissa croaked.

The orange light grew brighter and built to a steady flame, slowly creeping down the length of the steeple. Flaming embers dripped from the top into the thick crown, igniting small fires all around the highest parts of the tree.

"Crown fire!" a lumberjack shouted. "Clear out!"

A flaming branch near the top broke off, crashing through the branches, igniting more fires before flipping end over end for the final fifty feet and slamming into the ground. Bits of burning pine spread over the dry branches and twigs and logs scattered across the work site. The ground itself seemed to catch fire.

The narrow steeple at the top was now engulfed in fire, pitching forward with the wind. Then, with a sharp crack, the steeple broke free from the trunk below it, hurtling straight down at the girls.

Marissa and Clara dove to the side as the steeple crashed into the ground and exploded into a sizzling mass of sparks and fire. Marissa used the blanket to swat a red ember from her leg. She coughed as the burning pine smoke filled her mouth.

The way to the road was now blocked by a wall of fire, so Marissa and Clara ran in the opposite direction, up into the dark mountains. A violent crash made them look back as the branch Clara had been sitting on broke free and tumbled to the ground. More branches followed. The tree looked much shorter now, with fire reaching from every side, whipped by the high winds and reflecting in orange, red, and yellow on the storm clouds above.

They reached the edge of the valley and followed the path that Roosevelt and the Scottish man had taken, into the woods. Marissa looked over her shoulder at the Steeple Giant, now a lone, steady flame, like a sad birthday candle.

Lightning flashed. It began to snow. They crossed over the mountain ridge and into another valley. The fire was no longer visible behind them, but woodsmoke still clung to the air, and the clouds still glowed orange.

The snow in the air thickened and the wind accelerated. The orange clouds flickered white and thunder rolled across the hills. Marissa focused on the path ahead. She felt sick and useless. Lonely. Strange.

"That's enough," said Clara, collapsing against a rock.

They were in a small grove of giant sequoia trees, each one much smaller than the Steeple Giant. There was a shallow crevice in the base of one of the trees. Marissa settled into its meager shelter. Clara sullenly joined her. They huddled in silence beneath Sarah's blanket as night and snow continued to fall.

"We lost," said Clara finally.

Marissa closed her eyes. It hadn't seemed real. Now it did.

Marissa took a deep breath, and felt the cold sting of tears rolling down her cheeks.

"You're right," said Marissa out loud. "We lost."

"No," said Clara. "No, no, don't say I'm right. I don't want to be right."

"We lost," said Marissa. She felt like throwing up.

A distant lightning flash revealed the heavy snow still falling, burying the roots of the tall trees. She remembered what Sarah had said about the roots. They stand tall because they stand together. Marissa thought about her mom.

"But we have to keep fighting," said Marissa.

Clara shook her head. "You fight. I'm done."

Marissa squeezed her eyes shut and felt the hot tears cover her cheeks. She wanted to agree with her sister. She was thoroughly finished with it all. If it was all a game, she would have happily surrendered right then. But she knew she couldn't leave the game. She had to play the cards she'd been dealt.

Clara was soon snoring but Marissa couldn't sleep. She rested her head against the side of the crevice. She was cold. Wet. Hungry. Cramped. Tired. Still. A cold trickle of melting snow snaked down Marissa's neck. It reminded her of that night on the campaign in Minnesota.

Mom had taken so long to get in the door, shaking so many hands, smiling at so many people. The advance team should have planned a different way in for the family. Instead, Marissa and Clara were stuck in the freezing rain, waiting to get in under the awning. When they finally made it to the door, Marissa had to smile and wave as well, pretending she was excited and happy as the ice on her collar slowly melted and trickled down the back of her neck.

As Mom took the stage to the roars of the crowd, the girls followed a staffer into a small room off to the side of the gym. It was a coach's office, lined with pictures of Hibbing Community College women's basketball teams dating back to the 1970s. Trophies crowded the high shelf.

The staffer closed the door and left them alone. Marissa grabbed a napkin and tried to dry off her neck. Clara attacked the deli slices on the buffet with the same energy Mom was throwing into her remarks.

"They tell me it's time to give up," Mom's voice reverberated through the closed door.

"No!" shouted a woman in the crowd.

"They tell me the polls say I've got no chance!"

"Don't believe it!" yelled a man.

"But, my friends, let me ask you something. When the Hibbing Cardinals are down on that scoreboard up there, do they stop fighting?"

"No!" shouted the crowd.

Marissa and Clara exchanged amused looks. An hour ago it had been another gym in another town. Except that time it was the Cougars who never gave up.

"That's right," shouted Mom, "They fight harder!"

Clara started throwing punches at the air. Marissa laughed.

"And that's what we're gonna do!" Mom shouted. "You know, I've always believed that in order to get, you have to ask. And I want to get a better future for Hibbing, for Minnesota, for the United States of America! So I'm asking you to knock on every door! Call every voter! Win this thing!"

The crowd roared its approval. Marissa made a sandwich.

"I've never backed down from a fight," Mom shouted into the microphone. "When they tried to build a highway through my tree . . ."

Marissa's eyes snapped open. My tree?

CHAPTER 26

THE TUNNEL

THE bright morning sunlight surprised Marissa. A warm blanket of snow covered her legs. The air smelled clean and crisp. The sky was clear and blue. Not a trace of smoke or fire.

Why did Mom say "my tree"?

In all the times she'd heard the same speech, Marissa had never noticed that before.

Not "my trees."

Or "my forest."

My tree.

One tree.

Marissa ran her fingers over the wet wood.

What tree was Mom talking about? And what if she'd lost it, the way Marissa had just lost hers? What if that tree had been knocked down for a highway after all? Would Mom have kept fighting? Would she have become governor? President?

Probably. Mom never gave up on anything.

How exhausting that must be. What an impossible way to go through life.

Heavy footsteps crunched through the snow nearby.

"Die, gingerbread scum!" Clara mumbled in her sleep.

"Shh!" hissed Marissa.

"Weird dream," Clara said, opening her eyes.

Teddy Roosevelt's scowling face appeared in the crevice.

"Weirder reality," Clara said.

"I thought I smelled spies near my camp," said Roosevelt. "I wanted to be in the woods, entirely free of politics, and Alice sends her little mercenaries to keep an eye on me."

Marissa shook her head, feeling the frustration of the past twenty-four hours wash over her tired, hurting body. "You know, Mr. President," she said, "it's not always about you."

"Hear, hear!" shouted an unseen voice. The Scottish man strode into view, a wooden pipe clenched in his teeth.

"I did not ask for your opinion!" said Roosevelt.

"I offer it free of charge, Your Majesty," the Scottish man said with an exaggerated bow. "Now let us explore the wonders."

"What wonders?" asked Marissa, unfolding herself painfully from the crevice and standing in the snow. Clara groaned and crawled out after her.

Roosevelt and the Scottish man exchanged a knowing smile. Roosevelt used his big walking stick to pull back a pine branch, revealing a sunny gap in the trees.

Marissa walked through. And gasped.

She was on a cliff's edge, looking out over a steep canyon. One of the cliff faces looked like an upside-down bowl that was missing a side. Several waterfalls streaked down a jagged rock face farther down the valley, with curtains of mist floating out into the pink-and-orange sunrise. The tops of the canyon were white with snow, but far below, on the valley floor, was a rich green forest.

Marissa knew this place. "Yosemite," she breathed.

"The very one," said Roosevelt quietly. "It is . . ."—he shook his head, overcome with emotion—"unlike anything I've ever seen."

Roosevelt sat on the cliff's edge, legs dangling over the hundred-foot drop. He barely seemed to notice Marissa was even there. A condor with long black wings and fingertip feathers swooped past below them, circling over the green canyon floor.

"Last night I passed the most pleasant sleep of my life," said Roosevelt. "We camped on Glacier Point over there." He smiled. "I woke up buried in snow."

Marissa sat farther back from the cliff's edge, hugging her knees to her chest. Her night had not been pleasant. She was cold. Hungry. Tired.

The scene in front of her was beautiful, but her heart ached knowing they could chop it all down, dig it all up, burn it and flood it all they wanted. And there would be nothing left.

What would Mom do? She'd stop moping, for one thing. And she wouldn't be silent.

What would Alice do?

Who cared? Alice wasn't there.

Neither was Mom. Nor Dad. Nor Ethel or anyone else. Marissa knew it was just her and the president. He was in a position to do good things. And she was in a position to bug him.

In order to get, you have to ask.

"Mr. President," Marissa asked quietly, "will you let them destroy this valley too?"

"I am not here for a political discussion," said Roosevelt.

Marissa looked down at a section of clear-cut land on the valley floor, abandoned logs scattered by the creek.

I've never backed down from a fight.

"Yesterday you said you'd save my tree," said Marissa.

Roosevelt turned, the wind pressing the corners of his mustache against his cheeks. "Even I cannot stop lightning."

They tell me it's time to give up.

"Yeah, but did you mean it?" asked Marissa.

"When I pointed at that tree yesterday," said Roosevelt, "it was as good as saved."

"Well, maybe pointing at trees isn't enough," said Marissa.

Roosevelt ignored her. Then he pointed at the herd of sheep moving across the valley floor. "They are like locusts, consuming all in their path."

"Then do something about it," said Marissa. "Pass a law, do something that will last. Unless you're afraid of sheep."

Roosevelt sighed. "You are exceedingly truculent."

"I don't know what that word means," said Marissa. "But if it's good, I'm that."

Roosevelt picked up a pinecone and tossed it over the cliff's edge. "Leave me be."

"I will if you promise to do the right thing," said Marissa.

"Presidents don't always have the luxury of doing the right thing," said Roosevelt.

Marissa looked at him. "Dare greatly, Mr. President."

Roosevelt didn't answer. He didn't turn. He kept staring out at the open space in front of him. The waterfalls. The cliffs. The trees.

Marissa stood up and walked back into the woods. She found Clara chewing on a stick of beef jerky. The Scottish man had disappeared.

"He's getting the horses," Clara said with a full mouth. "Want some?" She broke off a piece of jerky and handed it to Marissa. "It's not chicken wings, but its OK."

Marissa chewed on the dried salted beef and looked around at the grove they'd slept in the night before. It was full of the same kind of trees as the Steeple Giant. Smaller, narrower, but still tall and mighty.

Some of them had advertisements nailed to their bark, close to the ground where passing tourists could see them. Notices. Leaflets. All flapping in the wind like feathers. Miracle cures and political candidates and train lines and San Francisco hotels all competed for space in the fluttering blizzard of paper, mostly yellowed, old and forgotten.

The Scottish man arrived with two horses.

Marissa looked out toward the cliff's edge. Roosevelt was still sitting there, looking out on Yosemite. As Marissa watched, he balled his fists and pounded them against his knees. His lips moved silently, and his hands flew out in intense gestures. He was debating something, arguing with the air.

When the sun was high, Roosevelt finally returned from the cliff's edge. He walked past the girls and the Scottish man, and went straight to the trees. He put his hand to the bark. He walked around them, reverently. He saw a flyer and angrily tore it off. He did the same with another, and another. Then he looked at the others.

"You people," he said, "are entirely too timid."

"Timid!" said Clara.

"Yes!" said Roosevelt. "Why push for one tree, one park, when there's a nation to save?"

He marched past them and prepared his saddle.

"So," said Marissa, "you're going to protect this land?"

"That's round one," said Roosevelt. "Then I'll move on to . . ."

"The Grand Canyon?" asked Clara.

"The Grand Canyon!" shouted Roosevelt.

"You might consider the Cascades to the north," the Scottish man suggested.

"The very thing," said Roosevelt. "The Black Hills of Dakota. Devil's Tower in Wyoming. A whole system of parks. To preserve in perpetuity!" He climbed into his saddle. "And every giant sequoia and bully redwood that's left in this magnificent nation. I've resolved to pick a fight with the interests and the scoundrels. There is no time to waste!" he said. "Let us pass laws and make enemies! Otherwise, what in blazes is the presidency for?"

A dull mist hung in the air as they descended from the mountains, swiftly making their way through the sweet-smelling woods, with Marissa riding with Roosevelt, and Clara with the Scottish man. After a few hours the smell gave way to lingering traces of smoke and ash. At the base of the mountain they reached a rocky clearing with a creek running through it.

On the other side, the desolation began.

The ground was black and crunchy underfoot, with the charcoal remains of trees and grasses that had lined the path. There were no signs of life anywhere. The only sound was the water of the creek passing along the scorched riverbank. There were no birds. No voices.

As they approached the burned remains of the Wendell Dam work site, Marissa braced herself. She didn't want to see the emptiness. When the horses reached the top of the ridge, she saw a little black column of bricks standing by the side of the creek. It was the chimney from Sarah's cabin. The rest of the cabin had burned away.

Marissa looked up the hill. And saw another black tower. Much taller. Charred, dark, lifeless and solitary. Shorter than it had been by about fifty feet, all of its branches gone. It looked like the Washington Monument had been painted black and abandoned.

But there it was, still standing.

"The Steeple Giant," Marissa whispered.

"Yes!" cried Roosevelt. He spurred their horse onward at a hard gallop. Roosevelt dismounted and ran to the blackened base of the tree.

"Yes," said Roosevelt as he ripped away the blackened bark between a pair of deeply charred roots.

"Yes!" he exclaimed again as he dug deeper into the tree, a small pile of black charcoal building behind him as he plunged farther into the tree's remains.

He emerged victorious, a handful of red bark in his hand.

"Extraordinary!" Roosevelt yelled. "A true exemplar of natural selection and horticultural resilience in the aftermath of catastrophe!"

"Um, what?" Marissa asked.

"He's saying it's alive!" Clara shouted joyfully as she jumped off the Scottish man's horse and ran to the tree, scrambling up a blackened root and getting soot all over her hands and clothes.

"How . . ." said Marissa, dismounting and cautiously approaching the tree.

The Scottish man scanned the top of the tree with his binoculars. "See here, Mr. President!"

Roosevelt dropped his handful of moist red bark on the ground and ran to take over the binoculars. Marissa picked up the bark and ran it through her fingers, marveling at how alive it felt. Marissa touched the tree and felt its energy. This tree was alive. She sat back against the trunk and closed her eyes. Listening to the creaking and moaning of the trunk.

Then an avalanche of soot rained down on her head. Marissa picked the debris out of her hair and looked up. Her sister was ten feet above, causing a mess as she tried to climb the loose black surface of the tree.

"There it is!" Roosevelt shouted in excitement, binoculars trained on the top of the trunk.

Marissa stood and walked over, the energy of the tree leaving her in a dreamlike trance. She took the brass binoculars and looked through. She had to adjust the focus. She looked up and down as the oily destruction loomed in clear magnification.

Then she saw green. All the way at the top, where the crown used to be, where the steeple-shaped spire used to rise, there was a tiny shoot of green poking out toward the sky.

"How is that possible?" asked Marissa.

"You don't live to be two thousand years old without a love of fire," explained the Scottish man. "She had two feet of bark to protect her from the flames."

Marissa understood. The lightning could rip away the steeple at the top. The fire could eat away all the piney branches. But the trunk was built to live. And now it was regenerating.

"And see here!" the Scottish man said, crawling around on the ground, getting black mud on his knees. "Look here!"

Marissa and Roosevelt joined him by a sooty patch next to a long, charred root. Peeking out of the ground, amid all the dead charcoal, was a little green stem, branching out into five bright green pine needles.

Marissa stood up and looked around. She was amazed that she hadn't seen it before. Amid all the black death were little signs of green life, poking through the layers of fire damage. All with the same little stem, and the same green needles.

Marissa pointed them out to the Scottish man. "Are those—"

"Tiny sequoia," he said with a smile. "Fire breaks the acorns. Feeds the soil. Opens a path for the sunlight and the water. Fire is an excellent gardener."

Marissa knelt down once more and touched the tiny plant. "So in a thousand years . . ." she said. She looked up into the highest reaches of the tree.

The Scottish man nodded. "In a thousand years, a mighty cathedral." He looked around. "Though it would only take about fifty years for this all to grow back to a decent little church."

"Marissa!" yelled Clara from the tree. "Check this out!"

Marissa ran over to find her sister on her hands and knees, disappearing through a dark triangular opening into the base of the tree. Marissa tucked the blanket under her arm and followed Clara through the opening and down the newly burned-out passage, all the way into the center of the tree. They were in a large chamber right in the middle that still smelled like fire and smoke.

Marissa knew right away. "I've been here before," she said.

"This wasn't here before!" Clara said. "It was carved by the fire!"

Marissa said nothing. She wrapped herself in the blanket and leaned against the moist wood. Exhaustion finally swept over her and she closed her eyes, listening to the tree that surrounded her, creaking, waving, whispering.

She felt refreshed and invigorated when Clara woke her up from her nap.

"Come on," said Clara. "They're heading for the train."

The girls hurried out of the tree and joined the president's traveling party. It was only later, when she boarded the train in Raymond, that Marissa realized she'd left the blanket in the middle of the tree. It was too late to go back. The train started chugging east the moment the president was on board.

Roosevelt was immediately on the move as well, marching up and down the train issuing directives and describing his conservation plans to anyone who would listen.

"He's finally acting like himself," observed Alice as she sat in the swaying baggage car, playing cards with Marissa and Clara. "How did you manage that?"

"I don't know," said Marissa, feeding a piece of bread to Josiah the badger through the bars of his wooden cage. "I think we just ticked him off enough."

The train ride home passed quickly. Even Mr. Loeb seemed to have made his peace with Marissa and Clara. He busied himself with putting the president's ideas into action, meeting with senators and congressmen to discuss new laws that would allow the president to create national monuments, forests, and parks.

With every stop, President Roosevelt talked more and more about caring for the land, and conserving for the future. He warned that without forests and meadows, the mountains would turn into deserts. He asked ranchers to limit their grazing, and loggers to cut in ways that would allow the forests to grow back. He talked to farmers about using water wisely, and described his plan to make the western lands bloom for generations.

Not everyone was happy to hear his message. But standing in those crowds, Marissa could see that he was changing the math, changing minds, changing the way the people thought about the land around them. His personality was so forceful, his words so convincing, and his dedication so real, they just had to listen. Alice had been right—it was in him all along, he just needed a push.

CHAPTER 27

HOME

WHEN the president's weary traveling party returned to the White House, Mr. Loeb opened the front door. The pony galloped out of the lobby to greet him.

"Loeb, I thought I told you to get that mule out of here," said Roosevelt, walking into the lobby and patting Algonquin affectionately.

"Father!" yelled Quentin from the top of the stairs. He slid down on a serving tray and leapt on Roosevelt's back.

Archie, now fully recovered from the measles, followed close behind.

"Hey, Archie, you wanted a souvenir," said Marissa. "How's this?" And she handed him the wooden cage with Josiah the badger.

Archie grinned and opened the cage. The badger scampered up the stairs. Somebody on the second floor screamed.

"You owe me money," said Ethel, standing behind Marissa.

"Oh no I don't," said Marissa, handing her an overstuffed purple sock. "We made it all back on the train ride home."

Ethel grinned. "Thank goodness for the press."

"Naw," said Marissa, "the reporters got too smart for us. We won this money off the senators."

"Hi, Clara!" shouted Quentin. "Let's climb a tree!"

Clara thought about the Steeple Giant and her stomach churned. "I think I've had enough tree climbing," she said.

Quentin looked disappointed. "But it's just a little tree," he said, pointing to the smallest tree on the lawn. "Father and I planted it last year."

Clara saw the tree he was talking about. It was a young oak with low-hanging branches that made it look like a little playground.

She agreed and they ran off to climb.

When she reached a sturdy branch near the top of the little tree, Clara said, "I have something for you."

She pulled out the iron pin that once held the caboose to the president's train. She put it in Quentin's hand. "You're the train expert," said Clara. "I thought you should have it."

Quentin stared in awe at the railroad artifact in his hand. "Thank you," he whispered.

He used the sharp end to carve his initials into the tree, then handed the pin back to Clara and pointed to a spot next to the Q and the R. Clara carved her initials C and S right next to it.

Then Archie came running across the lawn, yelling "Bear! Bear!"

Remembering the grizzly at Yellowstone, Clara instinctively gripped the tree. Then she saw President Roosevelt chasing Archie across the lawn, his face red, his big teeth clenched, and his fingers out like claws. Archie ran off giggling and Quentin sprang from the tree onto the president's back. With a roar, the president chased after one son, with another clinging to his neck. Ethel emerged from the bushes and tackled them all. Two dogs and a pig joined the fray.

Clara and Marissa watched as the president wrestled with his children. Then Roosevelt noticed them and said, "Ah, my daring troublemakers. Are you staying for dinner?"

Ethel answered for them. "No, Father, they have a fancy dinner of their own to go to."

"So," said Marissa, "that's it?"

"Mission accomplished, I would say," said Ethel. "I'd like my clothes back, please."

Clara and Marissa looked at the dresses they were wearing. "Yeah," said Marissa, "sorry for the mess."

"Life is messy," said Alice, briskly walking by on the sidewalk, barely seeming to notice the chaotic pile of humans and animals on the lawn. She paused to look at Marissa. "Don't ever let them keep you tidy."

"Change the math," Marissa responded.

"Always," said Alice. "Navy secretary meeting in five minutes, Father. If you're late, I'll name a battleship after myself."

"A fitting appellation indeed," Roosevelt responded grudgingly.

He lumbered to his feet and headed off toward the White House, face covered in dirt and sweat. Then he stopped and looked back at Clara and Marissa.

"Dare greatly," he said.

"Same to you!" shouted Clara.

Clara and Marissa changed into their old clothes in Ethel's room and headed to the State Dining Room. Clara crawled under the side table and gently pushed against the wing of the wooden eagle. The panel in the wall popped open.

Marissa followed her sister into the tunnel and down the spiraling slide.

When they reached the clubhouse, Marissa found matches and lit a candle.

"Look!" Clara shouted.

On the other side of the oval room, another door was open.

"I guess we accomplished the mission," said Marissa.

"Is that the way home?" asked Clara.

"It better be," said Marissa. "If we walk out into the Great Depression, I'm going to be really annoyed."

The girls stepped into the other tunnel. Marissa struggled up the slide as Clara waited impatiently below. Marissa reached the panel and pushed it open. She crawled out into the State Dining Room.

The animal heads were gone. The tables were back. Each was set with fine china, clean glasses, and little flags. The big hand on the grandfather clock was pointing at 12, and the little hand pointed to 4. No time had passed at all.

Just as Clara was about to crawl out through the panel, Big Dan walked around the corner. Marissa panicked and pushed against the panel with her knee, slamming it shut.

"Ow!" said Clara's voice through the panel.

Big Dan looked at Marissa curiously. "Are you OK, ma'am?"

"Yep! I'm great!" said Marissa. "Just hit my knee on the table. This used to be Teddy Roosevelt's table. Did you know that?"

"No, ma'am," he said. "Have you seen Sugar? She went in here a moment ago, and we heard a noise."

"Who, Clara?" said Marissa. "I can't keep track of that kid."

A waiter walked by carrying a silver tray with a large cover. He headed into the butler's pantry.

Marissa pointed at the closing door and said, "I think you better check that tray out. I thought I heard something moving under that cover."

"That's not funny, ma'am," said Big Dan.

"I mean, like," said Marissa, "I've heard of snakes getting in those, and whoa, is that embarrassing during a big dinner, you know?"

Big Dan gave her a look. "Snakes, ma'am?"

"Better safe than sorry!" said Marissa.

Big Dan shook his head. "Spot check on dining trays," he said into his sleeve, and walked into the butler's pantry.

"Thanks, Dan!" called Marissa. "You're the best!"

"Smooth," Clara whispered from behind the panel.

"Yeah, well, the coast is clear now," Marissa whispered back.

The panel swung open and Clara scurried out onto the floor. The girls ran through the lobby and up the stairs leading to their bedrooms. Clara searched the red carpet for pony prints, but all she found was a round serving tray covered with the remains of her dad's favorite roast beef sandwich. Apparently the girls weren't the only ones gearing up to deal with a long dinner.

As Marissa reached the top of the stairs, she saw a crumpled old blanket lying on the floor. Then she remembered how it all began—a hard kick of the soccer ball into the shelf, and the blanket came down.

At the bottom of the stairs she heard her mother's voice.

"So I meet with the leaders first, then we go into the dinner?" asked Mom, crossing the lobby downstairs.

"Yes, ma'am," said Stephanie, Mom's chief of staff.

Marissa grabbed the old blanket and quickly folded it. It felt fragile, with loose threads of brittle yarn. Then she noticed the pattern on the old blanket. A faded staircase.

"This speech lacks purpose," said Mom, looking down at her binder as she reached the top of the stairs. She wasn't watching where she was going and nearly crashed into Marissa.

"Mom!" said Marissa, giving her a tight hug, knocking both the binder and the blanket to the floor.

Footsteps thundered down the hall, then Clara slammed into the group hug as well. "Oh Mom, I missed you!"

Mom gave a surprised laugh. "Girls, it's only been—"

"It's been forever!" shouted Clara. "Can we get a pet?"

"What?" said Mom, surprised.

"Doesn't have to be a dog, could be like a badger or a hyena if you want. Or a pony."

"We can talk about a dog," said Mom. "Now, go get dressed, it's almost—"

"DINNERTIME!" Clara yelled enthusiastically. She cartwheeled down the hall. "I missed you, chicken wings!" she shouted. "I missed you, pizza!"

She stopped in front of her door. "Room!" she shouted. "I missed you, room!"

"We're not actually serving pizza, are we?" asked Mom.

"No, ma'am," said Stephanie, picking up the binder from the floor. "Menu for tonight is tab D." She picked up the old blanket and said, "I'll take this to housekeeping."

"No!" said Marissa and Mom at the same time. They both reached for the blanket, and Marissa got it first.

"Yes, ma'am," said Stephanie, eyebrows raised. She turned and started down the stairs. "I'll go talk to the speechwriters about . . . purpose."

Clara ran into her room and collapsed on her familiar bed, kicking her legs in the air. She flicked through the dresses in her closet and put on the first decent one she could find. As she dragged a brush through her hair, she looked out the window.

The old oak tree cast strange, dappled shadows over the South Lawn. Clara wished she could climb it with Quentin. Maybe she could have shown him the secret code she'd found carved up there. ORCS.

Then it hit her.

"It's a *Q*," she said out loud.

Quentin Roosevelt. Clara Suarez.

"It's not an O!" she shouted, running out into the hall, where Marissa and Mom were still standing. "It's a *Q*!"

"What?" asked Marissa.

Clara ran past and picked up Dad's serving tray. She dropped it at the top of the stairs and jumped on, sliding away. "Tell Dan I'm going tree climbing!" she shouted.

"At least she's dressed," Marissa said.

"Which is more than I can say for you," said Mom. "Can I have that blanket, please?"

Marissa turned the blanket over, slowly, feeling the brittle old fibers woven together, looking at the faded pattern. An even staircase of yellow and red and green.

"Give that to me now," said Mom. "Please."

The pattern was wrong in one place.

A horizontal yellow line extended an inch too far.

Mom's hand appeared on the blanket, gently trying to take it away.

Marissa held on tighter.

"Mom, what is this blanket?" Marissa asked, still clinging to the old blanket.

"You don't remember it?" asked Mom, still hanging on as well.

"No," said Marissa.

"We have pictures of you wrapped up in it," said Mom.

"This is my baby blanket?" asked Marissa in astonishment.

"For a time," said Mom. "But it belonged to me first."

"Where did you get it?" asked Marissa.

Mom took Marissa's hand. "Come," she said, leading the way into Marissa's bedroom.

"Madam President," said a staffer walking down the hall with a folder and a list.

"Not now," said Mom, firmly closing Marissa's door.

Mom sat on the bed and spread out the blanket. It was in worse shape than Marissa had realized. There were holes in it, and loose ends where the brittle yarn had separated. There was a black mark, from a long-ago burn. Marissa remembered the burning embers flying through the air. She remembered the blanket on her shoulders, covering her, protecting her.

Mom said, "I didn't get along with my parents, you know."

Marissa nodded carefully. This was not a topic they discussed often, but it was always there in the background. Mom's rotten childhood and how it made her president.

"Sometimes it got bad . . ." Mom said, her voice trailing away. She pulled the blanket close to her. "One time I ran away."

Marissa looked at her mother. "You never told me that."

"I didn't plan it," said Mom, "I didn't even pack, I just . . . ran into the mountains."

Marissa touched the blanket, remembering the cabin, remembering Sarah.

"It was stupid, I know," said Mom. "And it rained. But I found this tree, this giant tree, with a tunnel right through it. That's where I stayed. And sticking up from the ground in there was a corner of this blanket. It was so dirty and old, but . . . it was exactly what I needed to keep me warm when I needed it most."

Marissa said nothing, feeling a chill in her spine.

"If it wasn't for that tree," said her mom, "and this blanket . . ." Mom shook her head. "It sounds stupid, but it felt like someone had left it for me, to give me strength to go back home."

"So that's the tree you saved when they tried to build the road," said Marissa, lifting the blanket to her cheek.

"I didn't think you listened to my speeches," said Mom. "But yes, it was. I should show you sometime. It's hard to find, but it's up the hill from an old—"

"Chimney," said Marissa.

Mom looked at her, eyebrows up. "Yes. How did you know?"

"Can we go see the tree," asked Marissa, "next time you travel to California?"

Mom sighed. She sat up straight and looked like a president again. "You'll have to check with the travel office."

"Mom," said Marissa, "we're just going to sneak onto the plane if you say no."

Her mother gave her a wry smile. "All right, you may go on the next trip." She started for the door. "But first you have to get dressed for dinner."

Marissa collapsed on her bed. "I'm so tired," she said. "Do we really have to be there every time somebody visits our home?"

Marissa expected her mother to be angry. Instead she smiled.

"You know," Mom said, "we've been here three months and that's the first time I've heard you call this place home."

"Well," Marissa shrugged, "it is, isn't it?"

Mom took a deep breath and walked over to the window.

Marissa joined her. They could see the dinner guests lined up along 17th Street. Marissa noticed the branches shaking on the old oak tree on the South Lawn. Clara was visible near the top, running her finger over something in the bark, while Big Dan stood patiently below.

"The first time we had to send you off to school from here," said Mom, "I remember you both looking out the window of that black SUV with all those sirens and lights. And you waved goodbye. And as you pulled away with your own little motorcade, I asked myself, What have we done to these girls?"

"You took us on an amazing adventure," said Marissa. She smoothed the fold on her mother's dress. "Now get going. We've got work to do."

AUTHOR'S NOTE

White House Clubhouse is a work of fiction, but it is inspired by real people, in a real time and place.

Theodore Roosevelt was the twenty-sixth president of the United States, serving from September 14, 1901, until March 4, 1909. He and First Lady Edith Roosevelt shared the White House with six children—Alice, Ted, Kermit, Ethel, Archie, and Quentin. The White House had recently been renovated with its first elevator, and an expanded State Dining Room featuring a wooden eagle table that is still there today.

The Roosevelts brought an incredible collection of animals to the White House, including a hyena, six guinea pigs, a blue macaw, an owl, rabbits, and chickens. They had several horses, plus a pony named Algonquin, who was brought up in the elevator to cheer up Archie as he recovered from the measles. They also had a pet badger named Josiah, presented to the president by a girl in Kansas during his 1903 train trip west.

On that trip, Roosevelt spoke from the back of his train to adoring crowds across the country. Many of the speeches delivered by Roosevelt in this book quote directly from speeches he would deliver later in his career, including the 1908 Conference of Governors in which he warned against "the lavish use of our resources," and a 1910 speech in Osawatomie, Kansas, where he declared, "I recognize the right and duty of this generation to develop and use the natural resources of our land. But I do not recognize the right to waste them, or to rob, by wasteful use, the generations that come after us."

Roosevelt spent a lot of time in the woods on that 1903 trip, disappearing into the first national park, Yellowstone, for two full weeks. During that time, Roosevelt's personal secretary, William Loeb, was left behind in a train car in Cinnabar, Montana. Unlike in this book, this was Mr. Loeb's idea! He wanted to maintain a rolling White House office on a railroad siding while the president visited the park along with naturalist John Burroughs, one of the inspirations for the "Scottish man" character in this book. Also present for Roosevelt's Yellowstone visit was his old friend "Hell-Roaring" Bill Jones, the former sheriff of Billings County, Dakota Territory.

Another inspiration for the Scottish man is Sierra Club founder John Muir, whom Roosevelt would join for a camping trip in California's Yosemite Valley later in the same train trip. Muir used their journey through the valley as an opportunity to press for greater preservation of Yosemite and its surrounding land, and to promote the idea of a national network of parks and a federal agency to protect them. This would lead to the eventual creation of the National Park Service, and helped inspire Roosevelt's decision to create five new national parks and declare six national monuments, including Devil's Tower in Wyoming and the Grand Canyon in Arizona.

The partnership of Roosevelt with naturalists like Muir and Burroughs changed the way many people in the United States thought about environmental conservation, and their legacy lives on today in 423 national parks, monuments, and memorials. However, much of this preservation effort, and the writings of Muir and Roosevelt themselves, reflected a disregard for the first people who inhabited the lands that would eventually make up the national parks. Early conservationists tended to focus only on preserving the land, ignoring the rights and cultures of Indigenous peoples. In recent years, the National Park Service as well as other government organizations and preservation groups have taken steps to rectify these injustices, but much work remains.

President Theodore Roosevelt's legacy is not perfect, but his accomplishments helped shape the United States of today and provide an example for all who dare greatly in the cause of positive change for tomorrow. As he said in a speech in Paris in 1910, "It is not the critic who counts; not the man who points out how the strong man stumbles, or where the doer of deeds could have done them better. The credit belongs to the man who is actually in the arena, whose face is marred by dust and sweat and blood; who strives valiantly [. . .] and who at the worst, if he fails, at least fails while daring greatly, so that his place shall never be with those cold and timid souls who neither know victory nor defeat."

ACKNOWLEDGMENTS

This book was a group effort, with the best ideas coming from my children and coauthors, Jay and Clare. I am grateful for all of their writing, artwork, editorial feedback, and gentle prodding ("Daddy, where's the next chapter?"). I am also deeply grateful for the constant support and encouragement of my amazing wife Erin. I love you!

I thank my parents, Jill and John O'Brien, and my sisters Karen Cholewka and Jenny Fay, for bringing joy and inspiration into my life. Thanks also to Bill, Billy, Ella, and Holly Cholewka, Dave, Patrick, and Maureen Fay, Patricia, James, and Kate McNeece, Ian, Sean, and Eric Black, Jeanine Schoemaker, Lois Lewis, Mary, Joe, and Matthew McTernan, Mary Schiffer, and my entire family.

Guiding a rookie writer through the publishing process is no easy feat, and I thank my agent Reiko Davis, my editor Simon Boughton, publicist Megan Beatie, and illustrator Karyn Lee for all they have done to bring this story to life. I also thank everyone at Norton Young Readers, and at DeFiore & Company, for their dedicated support and belief in this project. I also want to thank the professionals who provided advice, read drafts, and kept me going, particularly Elizabeth Law, Peter Lerangis, Andrea Cascardi, David Kuhn, Jimmy Miller, Andrew Stuart, Matt Carmichael, Stew Shankman, Hopper Oehler, Jon Izenstark, and Alexandra Levit.

For this project, I relied on many sources for information and inspiration, including the writings of Theodore Roosevelt and

Alice Roosevelt Longworth, as well as some thrilling historical finds like Edith Roosevelt's hand-drawn plan for where the children would sleep in 1901. I am grateful to the White House Historical Association, the DC Public Library, the Library of Congress, the Theodore Roosevelt Center at Dickinson State University, and the National Park Service for access to these materials. I also owe a debt of gratitude to several historians for their comprehensive histories of Theodore Roosevelt, including *Theodore Rex* by Edmund Morris and *The Wilderness Warrior* by Douglas Brinkley, as well as the many historians who contributed to the Ken Burns series *The Roosevelts: An Intimate History.*

I want to thank all who helped build my journey as a writer, from mentors like Ellen Turner, Bob Blackwell, Bernie Robinson, Alicia Smith, Mick Napier, Judy Schneider, and Shailagh Murray, to the many great speechwriters and communications professionals I've worked with on Capitol Hill, the White House, the Pentagon, and Georgetown University. I thank all of the teachers I've had, from PS 166 to the Center School, Cathedral, Stuyvesant, and Northwestern, as well Jay and Clare's teachers at Peabody, Watkins, and BASIS DC.

Finally, a word of thanks for the leaders who have trusted me to help craft their voice as they continued Theodore Roosevelt's legacy of public service, including Congressmen Quigley, Foster, and Shuler, Ambassadors Emanuel and Braithwaite, Secretaries Carter, Spencer, Modly, McPherson, Harker, and Del Toro, First Lady Dr. Jill Biden, and President Joseph R. Biden.